# UNREADABLE

AN ACTION ADVENTURE ROMANCE

THE UNDERCOVER FILES
BOOK 1

## TROY LAMBERT

## CJ RIZK

Unreadable

Copyright © 2024 by Troy Lambert and CJ Rizk

All rights reserved.

No part of this book may be reproduced in any form or by any electronic or mechanical means, including information storage and retrieval systems, without written permission from the author, except for the use of brief quotations in a book review.

## CHAPTER ONE
### HARPER

I GAZED through the rain-spattered window of my Uber as it came to a stop in front of a hotel that looked a lot more opulent than I'd expected.

The newspaper I worked for wasn't exactly rolling in dough, and my boss, Sal, was a notorious cheapskate. He'd booked me in more than a few roach motels in the year since he'd hired me, claiming that all a real journalist needed was cheap coffee, a bed, and a pack of cigarettes.

A generous benefactor of the written word, he was not.

So this swanky place was a freaking godsend.

Despite the sweet digs, a knot of apprehension tightened my stomach as I stepped out of the Uber. The salty Galveston air did zilch to quiet my nerves, and that had nothing to do with my typical unease of being in a new place on a consistent basis.

It was the nagging sense of failure that had dogged my heels since my fall from grace. My promising career in investigative journalism had bombed in an epic way, and instead of covering the high-profile stories my father would have salivated over, I was here.

In Galveston.

About to cover a kiddie sandcastle competition.

A far cry from the high-stakes reporting I used to do.

"You pay?" the Uber driver asked as he rolled my suitcase to the curb.

He barely looked street legal, but his age and how he got his license were none of my business.

I stared at him for a second before what he'd said registered. "It's an Uber app, kid. You know how those things work, right?"

His bland expression told me he loved his job about as much as I did. He waited me out for an awkward beat, then he held out his hand, rubbing his thumb and forefinger together.

"Dude, I tip you on the app."

"You say that, but no one ever does."

I wasn't surprised. Not one for motion sickness, I'd still been ready to lose my ill-advised breakfast after a few minutes of his jerky bobbing and weaving.

The kid drove like he was being tasered.

Conscious of the pouring rain, and the fact that we were now drenched, I shrugged my shoulders and reached for some cash in my back pocket. He'd called me out on my bullshit, and I respected that.

"What's your name?" I asked.

"Jeffey Mikey."

"Okay, Jeffey Mikey. Can I just call you Mikey?"

"Knock yourself out."

A near smile made my lips twitch.

I liked this kid.

"Can you be back here in about two hours to take me to the sandcastle competition?"

"Rough social life? That event is for like…five-year-olds."

I hated this kid.

"You wanna make money or not?"

His head nodded vigorously. "I'll be back in two hours. But with this rain, it might get canceled."

*Dear God, if only.*

I watched him hustle to his car, his skinny frame and short legs making me think he couldn't be older than thirteen, but what the hell did I know?

Dragging my suitcase behind me, I entered the hotel lobby a soaking mess and headed straight for the front desk. The place managed to be extravagant and welcoming with its coastal-themed decor.

But I shivered with unease anyway.

The clerk was busy on the phone, giving me a moment to take in the grand staircase and the tastefully arranged seating areas. It was then that I noticed him. The man seemed oddly out of place among the hustle and bustle of guests and staff.

He sat at the hotel bar, reading a physical newspaper, of all things. Despite my profession, it wasn't something I saw every day.

I stared at him unabashedly, analyzing his impressive attire and wishing that damn paper didn't block his face. I planned on locking away the visual details for later. While I never trusted my initial impressions of someone, clothing spoke volumes.

He wore a tailored charcoal, slim-fit suit that hugged his broad shoulders. A Tom Ford…maybe Brioni. High-end brands like that spoke of a dude meticulous about outward appearance, not to mention control issues. His crisp, bespoke dress shirt and polished leather Oxfords made me wanna barf.

And that black briefcase? Louis Vuitton, if I knew my elitist brands.

And I did.

Guess no one shopped at Walmart these days.

He was definitely put together, and I had to wonder if this fashionable show of power signaled hierarchy. What corporate cesspool did this dude lord over?

And why the hell did I care?

A moment of familiarity struck me. Not that I recognized him, but I recognized the annoyance I felt at taking note of him and that uncomfortable tearing sensation in my chest, looking at someone I didn't want to want.

The only time I'd ever had an internal battle of that magnitude was in prep school with Miles Westbrook.

Elitist asshole extraordinaire.

And currently, a criminal running a criminal empire…although no one ever believed me on that last part.

I shivered at the thought, having thoroughly spooked myself.

"Welcome to the Seagate Hotel. How may I assist you?" The clerk, now off the phone, startled me out of my scrutiny.

"Harper Quinn. I have a reservation," I replied, ignoring the way the clerk stared at my bedraggled state.

Yeah. I got it. Most of the guests around here were dressed to the nines, oozing money and a severe superiority complex.

What the hell was Sal thinking booking me here?

"Oh, yes, Ms. Quinn. We have you in a sea-view room. I hope it meets your expectations." He handed me the key card.

A sea-view room?

Screamed expensive, which threw me. I got the distinct impression that I was being punked.

I thanked him and headed to the elevator, taking it to the sixth floor, my mind still on the man at the bar. His presence nagged at me, an itch I couldn't quite scratch.

It was only when I reached my room and wheeled my suitcase inside that the full weight of my surroundings hit me. On the desk, a pamphlet boasted the hotel's amenities, the logo proclaiming, "A Westbrook-owned Franchise."

My heart sank.

Westbrook!

This hotel was owned by the Westbrooks?

The realization stung. I pulled out my phone, dialing my boss with shaking fingers, needing someone to blame.

"Yeah," was his curt greeting.

"Sal, you booked me into a Westbrook hotel? Are you trying to get me killed?"

"Harper, calm down." The sound of his smoke-ridden lungs coughing up phlegm made my nausea return. "I didn't—look, it was the only place with a vacancy that fit the budget."

"Fit the budget? Are you insane? This room is at least three times the rate you're usually willing to shell out. So tell me the truth."

A heavy sigh crackled over the line. "Your father called me. He's in the area, and he wanted to meet you for drinks. He booked the hotel."

All the air left my lungs.

I hadn't spoken a word to my father in over a year. Though, to be honest, I'd hardly had much to do with him since the day he'd moved in with his mistress and left me and Mom in the lurch. He'd tried to reach out a time or two, but I was a vindictive bitch, prone to grudge-holding. And even though his connections in journalistic circles would have easily helped me climb my career ladder, I'd fought for every single promotion I'd ever gotten.

I took nothing from him. Accepted nothing from him.

And this passive-aggressive shit was so like him. The fact that he had insisted on meeting me here at a Westbrook-owned hotel, of all places, wasn't just about meeting me because he cared or pretended to care. He was making a point. Rubbing all my claims—all the shit that went down a year ago—in my wounds as a way to make me deal with reality and no doubt my fears, even if he didn't think they were valid.

It was a blatant slap in the face.

"You know your situation. After your…let's call it a mishap… your father reaching out seemed like a good break for you, kid. He might be able to help you get your career back." His voice was a mix of impatience and faux sympathy.

"How much did he pay you to set this up?"

"Now, Harper—"

"Sal, my mishap was an attempted murder. My car's brakes didn't just happen to malfunction all on their own."

"They didn't malfunction at all. You know what the inspector said."

"And," I continued, his comment fueling my rage, "I was not voluntarily under the influence of *anything* when this alleged accident occurred. I was set up, Sal! And I'm tired of everyone, including my own father, minimizing and dismissing the very real corruption surrounding the Westbrooks, not to mention their attack on *my* life."

"You got no proof, Harper. And you sound crazy as—"

"Call me crazy one more time, and I'll write up a story on how sandcastle competitions for five-year-olds are a health hazard. Those kids might as well be playing in kitty litter."

"Harper, listen to me. You're lucky to have any job in journalism at all after the stunt you pulled. Just do the assignment, keep your head down, and maybe, just maybe, we can start rebuilding your career."

His words doused me like a bucket of ice water, and all my fire sputtered out. I was too much of a liability now, and too much of a risk.

A year ago, I was on the verge of uncovering one of the biggest scandals in Texas politics—until my informant was killed. On the heels of that injustice, I'd nearly lost my life in what everyone else wrote off as a tragic DUI, which then cost me my job.

*My informant.*

I shoved thoughts of her aside, not willing to revisit that horrific night.

Only I knew the truth about the Westbrooks' involvement, but with no proof and no platform, my accusations sounded like the bitter grumblings of a disgraced reporter.

"Just fix this shit with your dad. He's your only hope of recovering what you've lost here."

"Sounds like you're ready to fire me too, Sal."

His heavy cough sounded more like a dry heave. "Stay or leave. I don't really care, but your dad scares me. If he wants you working for him, I won't stop you. You're free to go."

"I can assure you, the last thing dear old dad wants is me working for him."

Hanging up, I felt the familiar tug of worry for my mom, which happened all day, every day, but especially after any mention or reminder of my asshole father. I quickly called her, anxious to hear her voice and praying it would sound sober.

"Mom, it's me. Just checking in. How are you today?"

"Oh, Harper, dear. I'm fine, really. Just reading a bit. You ever gonna call me without sounding like you're bracing for an explosion?"

I rubbed my tired eyes and slowly let out a breath. She sounded good. Good enough, all things considered.

"Sorry, Mom. Old habits and all."

"How's Galveston? Did you see the beach yet?"

Her voice was light, but it carried that edge of fragility that had become more pronounced since Dad's affair with my English teacher—a revelation that had sent her spiraling back into her old, destructive habits.

Habits that she'd had to claw her way through. With me by her side, helping her. Always helping her.

"It's…uh, it's nice, Mom. You took your meds today?"

"I did, sweetheart. Just try to take care of yourself for once. When you're finished with your assignment, go to a spa. Treat yourself. Relax a little. You're in your late twenties, for god's sake. Get laid or something."

I laughed out loud, surprised at how good it felt and how much I needed it. "I don't have time to get laid."

"Yeah. That concerns me. You deserve to have some fun."

"I'll work on fun as long as you work on your meditations for the day."

She chuckled, sounding better than she had in a while. "I'll do that. My mind wanders, though. You know how it is."

"Look, just remember what Dr. Steiner said, okay? One day at a time," I replied, my voice softening.

We talked a little more about trivial things—her book club, her eccentric neighbors—before saying goodbye. I hated that I couldn't be there to make sure she was truly okay, but this assignment, as ridiculous as it seemed, was how I currently paid the bills.

Student loans were a bitch, and Mom's healthcare wasn't cheap either.

I checked the time, realizing that our chat had taken longer than expected. I hurried and showered, washing all thoughts of my father down the drain. He wasn't worthy of the mental space.

By the time half-past three hit, I was in the lobby and heading for the double doors, feeling an unreasonable sense of vulnerability now that I knew a Westbrook might be in the area. Thank god I had my handgun in my purse. It was Texas, after all.

Still, that handgun didn't dismiss the sensation of being watched. The paranoia that comes with what I'd dubbed SDS—Sitting Duck Syndrome—just waiting for someone to take you out.

It'd been a year since I'd experienced that level of fear. I cursed my father for putting me in this position, but it made no difference. I wouldn't get an ounce of sleep in this place now that I knew who owned it.

I stared at the slightly overcast sky as I exited the building. The rain had stopped.

A damn shame.

Mikey sat on the hood of his clunky Honda Civic, trying to exude an air of maturity that failed to hit the mark since he looked like he was swimming in hand-me-downs from a linebacker-sized older brother.

"You ready, kid?"

He nodded and circled to the driver's side while I hopped in the back. I barely had my seat belt on before he peeled out, leaving the sound of squealing tires in our wake.

"Dear Lord, who the hell taught you how to drive?"

"Why would anyone have *taught* me?"

Yeah. That explained a few things.

# CHAPTER TWO
## MILES

EVERY STEP HURT as I entered the lobby of the Seabrook Hotel, my hotel. The one I manage, at least. I didn't even have a good story to go with my twisted ankle. Just a step back onto a weight plate carelessly left on the floor of the gym, likely by one of the rich assholes staying here.

Getting dressed after my workout was painful, but I couldn't be seen in anything less than my best—Daddy's orders.

It still infuriated me that while I managed all the day-to-day operations, my dad technically owned the hotel. He was a congressional representative which should have told me everything I needed to know about his integrity, but I'd been in denial about his business for a long time.

Not anymore.

I loved it here, though. Galveston. I loved this building, too. It was one of a kind, rising from the island mere steps from the beach. Almost all the rooms have amazing views, many of them with sea views that draw wealthy vacationers and business travelers alike.

None of them matched mine from the penthouse, but a few came close.

It was raining, which ~~kind of~~ spoiled the view, but forecasters said it would clear in an hour or two. They were usually pretty accurate around here. All the rounds of hurricanes and storms made them hyper-vigilant, even when it came to everyday weather events.

As much as I loved it here, this was not where I wanted to be. But sometimes your choices were made for you, like blowing out your knee in your last college game, dashing your NFL hopes.

Something like that.

I limped my way to the bar in the lobby, watching the line of well-dressed travelers checking in. Most smiled, a few frowned, and some were deep in conversation.

"Drink, Westbrook?" Jordan Kant, my best friend, hospitality manager, and also one of the best bartenders in Galveston, asked me. I played college football with Jordan, who, at nearly six and a half feet tall, dwarfed my six-foot frame. He was much more muscular than me. Jordan was one of the best cornerbacks at Texas A&M until he got one too many concussions his senior year. You could say we'd both missed the NFL by only a few yards. I was a kicker, so it was more like one field goal.

That injury ended my dreams of leaving the family business and having a long NFL career. Jordan still called me by my last name most of the time, and so I did the same to him.

"Just orange juice today, Kant. And the paper."

"You know you can read the paper on your phone now? Save a tree?" The Galveston County News hit the bar, though, and in what seemed like a second, a large glass of orange juice appeared beside it, resting on a coaster decorated with a giant "W."

*God, I hate those coasters.*

"I know I could," I said. "But you don't read the oldest newspaper in Texas on a tablet."

"You don't read anything on a tablet."

It was true. I usually carried a paperback with me everywhere. Sometimes two if I was reading non-fiction at the same time as a novel.

"I know e-readers exist," I told him. "And that I can hold my entire library in one, but I prefer physical books."

*And vinyl over digital music. Cable over streaming. For a guy nearing thirty, I really do feel like an old soul.*

I swiveled to the side of my bar chair so I could stretch my leg a bit, rubbing my sore knee. I opened the paper but looked up sharply.

A woman in line at the front desk caught my attention. I silently wished she would turn so I could see her face.

She didn't fit the typical profile of the guests here. Her hair was a mess, her clothing damp and wrinkled, and not entirely because of the rain.

The almost recognition wasn't comfortable. Like seeing an old friend or an ex-lover. Not that I had many of those. I should know her, but I felt a tiny, odd twinge of fear at even the prospect of discovering who she was. So I looked at her out of the corner of my eye, keeping my face behind the paper. I wanted to recognize her before she recognized me.

That didn't make any sense, and intellectually I could see that. But feelings overrode the brain from time to time.

*Maybe I should just go over there, tap her on the shoulder, and see what happens.*

"Someone you know?" Kant asked, echoing my thoughts.

"No. Maybe. I'm not sure."

"Scorned lover? Someone's wife you should have stayed away from?"

"No, she's—"

"Hey, bro!" a voice came from behind me, and I cringed and turned around.

"Reanne? What are you doing here?"

"Is that any way to greet your sister?" My sister, a fiery redhead, wore her hair pulled up tightly in a top bun. Today, she had on a forest green blazer over a low-cut tan blouse, a pencil skirt that matched the blazer, and sensible black heels. Her attire was clearly

Daddy-approved, too, and far from the goth wear of her teenage years and her early twenties.

Left to her own devices, she was anything but sensible.

"Hi, Jordan," she almost sang. "Are we talking about one of your many admirers?"

"No, we're—" I turned toward the front desk, but the woman was gone.

Reanne stared at me, her green eyes sparkling.

"Never mind," I covered quickly. "I thought I saw someone I knew."

"Jordan," she said, moving past me. "Are you seeing anyone?"

"No," the bartender replied with a grimace. "Not at the moment."

"Are you free later? I'd love to have dinner and catch up." Reanne winked at him, and I threw up in my mouth a little.

"Afraid not," Jordan said. "I've got a family dinner to go to."

"Another time, then."

"Reanne," I said, taking hold of her shoulders and staring right at her. "What are you doing here?"

"Just a little trip to see how you are doing and to soak up some sun." She gestured outside, where the rain had slowed to a drizzle.

"Sure. Who is taking care of the place in Austin?"

"Cynthia."

"Your best friend, Cynthia? Is she even…"

"She's been clean for six years, Jar. Her biggest vice now is those damn brownies she is always making. Get over it."

I hated that nickname. "Does Dad know you're here, and that you left her in charge?"

"He not only knows, but he told me it was a great idea."

"Really?" My stomach rolled. Her timing could not be worse.

Just then, my phone chirped in my pocket.

I pulled it out.

*Damn, wrong phone.*

The chirp came from my other one.

"Uh, sorry," I heard myself stammer. "I have to take this. I'll catch you later, Reanne?"

"Dinner?"

"Sure," I responded without thinking. "See you at seven."

Instead of heading to my office or my room, which seemed like a long way away, I moved toward the front door and stepped outside.

I looked around to make sure no one had noticed me, pulled a second phone from my other pocket, and flipped it open. The text had three numbers and one word.

Ace.

I typed two numbers and hit send. The rain had passed, and the sun emerged, pleasantly warming the air with that after-shower smell. Though that would normally cheer me up, it didn't. That sun represented hope, and any hope I'd had for today had just been dashed into nothingness.

I'd have to keep my dinner with Reanne short. Some appointments couldn't be broken.

As I headed back inside, I thought again of the woman in line. I'd have to find her later and figure out how we knew each other. It should be easy since she was staying here.

As I entered the lobby, I saw the shock of Reanne's hair entering the elevator. So I turned and limped back to the bar, cursing my bad knee and twisted ankle, grabbed the paper, and headed for my downstairs office.

I could get a little work done, at least. Maybe tomorrow, I would spend some time out by the pool.

# CHAPTER THREE
## MILES

*Six Hours Later*

"WELP, it's been nice catching up. I gotta go." I casually wiped my chin, folded my napkin, and moved to stand.

"Go? The night is young," Reanne said. "You're just going to leave me all alone?"

"You have friends here, and you can make new ones," I said, pointing to a group of women who had just walked into the restaurant. They were all dressed to go out, probably for the club scene, and were laughing and joking, all while texting, too.

"What do you have to do right now?"

"I've got a meeting," I told her.

"A meeting? Really? What's her name?" Reanne sipped her drink and sneered up at me.

"Not her, him."

"Whatever floats your boat. Nice to see you coming out."

"C'mon, Reanne. It's business."

"Got it. Well, text later if you don't want to miss all the fun."

"Will do."

By the time I got away from my sister and outside the

restaurant, I felt like I was late. And I was, by a whopping fifteen minutes. I had to hope my handler would wait.

I walked as fast as I could down the street, sending my injured ankle into misery, swerving around pedestrians and tourists, and heading toward the beach.

I stopped and sat on a bench near the fishing pier, taking deep, slow breaths.

And I waited. Someone should have come. I checked my secondary phone again. Nothing. No messages and no calls asking where I was.

I set a timer on my watch for fifteen minutes. I'd wait as long as I'd made them wait.

As I sat, I stared out at the gulf and the waves crashing against the beach. The water there gave life and took it away so easily. What was I doing anyway? Without the information from my handler, I couldn't fulfill my end of the bargain with the FBI.

It sure didn't feel like betraying my family was any kind of bargain. But I couldn't go on living, knowing what I knew without doing something.

And this was something. But without the right codes to access the information my contact at the FBI needed—and without a way to transmit it to him—I couldn't do anything at all.

Maybe they changed their minds. Maybe they found someone else, some other way to get to my father.

Maybe that wouldn't be such a bad thing. My dad could never know I betrayed him, even if he lost his seat in Congress and went to jail for a hundred years.

A feeling came over me then. Someone was watching me. Maybe even waiting for me. I couldn't stay here any longer.

Just as I stood, my timer went off.

I turned and made my way back to the hotel as quickly as possible, my ankle and knee screaming in protest. I slowed near the entrance, limping past the doorman. The entire time, I couldn't shake the feeling that I was being followed.

"Evening, Ed."

"Evening," Ed said. He wore an expensive suit and tie nearly as nice as mine. A hotel perk. My father insisted that Westbrook doormen were not to look like doormen did everywhere else. "Everything alright, sir?"

"Yes, just in a bit of a hurry." I pushed past him.

I went into my office and found it empty. Everything looked just as I'd left it this afternoon—nothing out of place.

I walked to the shelf behind the enormous oak desk, picked up a football encased in glass. I turned it over and removed a tiny brown envelope taped to the bottom.

Without my handler, I couldn't do anything more with this. I decided to see if I could spot who might have been following me. I took off my suit jacket and shirt, hanging them on the coat rack behind my desk. After putting on a baseball cap, I slid on a flannel over my dark t-shirt, and stepped out of my office, face pointed at the ground.

I hurried to the bar, looking around as I went.

I stepped up, thinking of signaling Jordan, but he was occupied with a customer. Then I saw her, down by the bar—the woman from earlier.

And this time, I did recognize her.

*Harper Quinn.*

And in the corner of the bar, Reanne sat in a booth with a gaggle of friends. She waved.

Shit. I did not want my sister to see Harper here.

Harper chatted with a few women, laughing and giggling. They all sounded drunk.

Hell, if I'd been through what she'd been through, and at the hands of my own family, no less, I would have been drinking night and day.

*It's a wonder I'm not.*

But her being here couldn't be a coincidence. Why would she be here if she wasn't investigating again? She could be in real danger. What in the world could she be thinking?

Things had just gone from bad to worse. I'd have to keep an eye on her and my sister. But how would I manage that?

Jordan approached her group, and I listened, keeping my head turned and my face down, hopefully in shadow. I heard Harper ask loudly, "Is there a tattoo shop near here?"

Relief hit me hard as I watched Harper leave the bar with the group, clocking her movements and Reanne's activities back and forth, hoping Harper got out of there before my spiteful sister recognized her. Because there was history there that went beyond the fallout of Harper's investigations over a year ago.

I slipped off the bar stool and headed for the door. I needed a drink, but not here. There was plenty of fine booze in the penthouse bar where I could be alone with my thoughts.

I waited, restless. I read a book and reviewed some budget numbers, but they all blurred together. Desperate, I turned on the rarely used television in my office and streamed a BBQ cooking show—not that I was all that interested, I just needed the visual and audio distraction.

At first, I checked both phones every ten minutes, and then every five. By eleven, I'd heard nothing on either phone. I should have gone to bed, but instead, I lay down on the couch and flipped the television toward me, closing my eyes for just a second, or so it seemed.

I woke up to a quiet ping from the burner phone still lying on my chest.

I flipped it open to read the text from my handler, and all the breath left my body.

Find Harper Quinn

## CHAPTER FOUR
### HARPER

I WOKE up groggy and disoriented, feeling the familiar regret that comes with pounding several shots of tequila too fast. I blinked bleary eyes and glared at the sliver of offending sunlight seeping through the window shade. The shade itself had somehow maneuvered in such a way that allowed said sunlight to hit me square in the eyes.

The nerve.

"Why?" I mumbled to no one, shoving myself up and onto my elbows.

My pounding head did not like this at all.

When I finally got into a seated position and looked around my hotel room, my eyes widened in shock.

A bomb had gone off! One filled with party favors, plushy toys, and bright pink and blue streamers. My brain cataloged the details on autopilot, knowing that getting them right the first time was always a good way to salvage a particularly slippery story.

Not that this was a story worth reporting, but old habits do die hard.

I numbered the details in my head, feeling more confused by the second.

One: A half-eaten kebab on the floor next to the bed. Strange, since I wasn't particularly partial to kebabs.

Two: A few of my most suggestive panties hanging from the bedpost. What the actual fuck?

Three: Prickly pain in my left shoulder. I'd deal with that one later.

Four: Eighty-seven stuffed rabbit toys, all in different shapes and sizes, covering the floor and the bed, flung around the place in careless heaps. Fine, maybe it wasn't eighty-seven, but I loved a good odd number.

Five: A dark, gaping hole in my memory of last night that reeked far worse than just tequila.

I tried to reason it all out but gave up for the moment, knowing the slightest hint of coherent thought would make my aching head retaliate with vindictive force.

I stood unsteadily and reached for the blinds while groping for the nightstand. I knocked over a gaggle of soft rabbit toys in the process. These little bastards were where my painkillers should have been.

The movement made my shoulder hurt like a bitch.

"Doggone it," I hissed.

I attempted a slow glide to the bathroom, but I slipped on a stupid fucking rabbit and fell flat on my ass. The toy making a squeaking noise added insult to injury.

"Fuuuuuck!"

I remained sprawled on the floor in the fluffy mess and pinched the bridge of my nose. I needed to piece together the details of what had happened last night and find out just how out of control I'd allowed myself to be. Obviously, my mom wasn't the only one who lost it when she drank.

I'd learned from the best.

But I didn't have a lot of pieces to work with. I thought back to the suicide drive through Galveston with Mikey at the wheel.

Thrill seekers beware.

Adrenaline had nothing on that kid.

I'd gone straight to the beach, with Mikey deciding to park and follow. We'd stood in solidarity, resigned to watch a slew of snot-nosed children jump around technicolor plastic structures while shoveling sand into just about anything other than where the sand was meant to go .

After seeing one kid scoop it into his mouth and another dump sand down the front of his pants, I'd decided my career had most definitely hit rock bottom. I planned on drinking myself to death that very evening.

Mission nearly accomplished.

Mikey had remained silent at my side. A detached expression on his face. This kid had seen things. A sandcastle competition like this shit show was mere child's play for him.

Literally.

Like any good journalist, I'd stifled my instinct to strangulate everything that resembled a neck.

The PR manager for the event had approached me. We'd put on our best fake smiles, as only southern women knew how, and exchanged empty pleasantries.

Whenever a toddler stumbled and fell, we'd both lay a fanned hand over our chests and sigh, "Oh, ain't that cute," while my Uber driver died of boredom.

After the competition, Mikey took me to grab some coffee. By that point, I was feeling like a rolled-over bird.

"How do you take it?" he'd asked.

"How do you take yours?" I'd genuinely wanted to know something about the kid before he crashed the car and killed us both .

"Coffee tastes like tar and stunts your growth."

Since I had no witty response for that, and it was silently understood that the kid desperately needed a growth spurt, I'd told him to grab me a shot of espresso from the nearest Starbucks. He dropped me off at the hotel where he'd received another generous tip, and then he was gone— leaving the smell of burned rubber something to remember him by.

I'd entered the bar with my laptop bag over my shoulder and found a spot to work. I furiously typed up what I promised would be my last hack job because this was not why I'd become a journalist.

After that, I'd dropped off my computer in the hotel room and returned to the bar, determined to make several bad choices before my dad finally flagged me down and forced me to talk to him. The bartender, a nice, smiley giant of a guy named Jordan, was most accommodating. He handed me drink after drink and introduced me to more people at the bar.

That was it. That was all I could recall.

All of it was seriously unhelpful.

The logistics of the whole thing got to me. How was I gonna get rid of what looked like evidence of some kinky furry party? And who the fuck did I celebrate with?

I needed to know what the hell had happened last night. Deciding I was too much of a hazard to myself when upright, I stayed on the floor and reached for my purse next to the nightstand. My phone was as good a place as any to start.

I was a maniacal party photographer. Call it my reporter instincts. There was sure to be a miniature photo essay of whatever had happened last night.

I turned the phone on and went straight to my pics.

Empty.

I didn't know what to make of this. Someone had deleted all of my photos and not just those from the night before.

"The plot thickens," I mumbled.

Because even in my most inebriated state, I never would have deleted pics on my phone. I was too hard-wired to keep evidence, no matter what it revealed.

The constant burning of my shoulder told me to sit up and do something about it. Maybe splash some water on my face and grab some hotel coffee. The mundane might jar something.

I succeeded in getting to my feet and shuffled like a zombie—or maybe a corpse—to the bathroom sink.

My reflection startled me. My hair frizzed out of my skull, looking like a million black baby thunderbolts. My mascara was everywhere else *except* my eyelashes, and my eyes were red and bloodshot, making the hazel look otherworldly. What a sorry, sorry spectacle. And…*ouch!* My shoulder burned like a bitch.

But burning shoulders, unlike kebabs, streamers, and far-flung panties, were not atypical features of my hung-over mornings. I inched closer to the mirror and angled my shoulder forward, noting some redness and irritation. I took off my white tank top to get a better look.

Slowly, I turned my body around. With my eyes fixed on the mirror I braced myself for a terrible gash, or a monster mosquito bite, or maybe a…

Noooooo.

No fucking way!

Sprawling from the back of my shoulder, all across my shoulder blade was black ink that ran up and down my skin.

*My god. A tattoo.*

And not just *any* tattoo.

The most fucking awful tattoo I had ever seen in my life.

Jordan approached me with a big smile on his face as I carefully settled myself on a barstool.

"How are we doing today, Harper?" He looked me over, his amusement plain as day.

"This is all your fault," I said.

He raised his hands and shrugged his shoulders. "I am merely at your service, here to make sure I get you everything you require."

"Did I require the mother of all hangovers?"

He chuckled. "I didn't say I was responsible for the consequences. But I may have a remedy."

"I'll take that remedy and any knowledge you have regarding what exactly happened last night."

He made quick work of a beverage that looked all kinds of foreign to me. When he set the drink in front of me, I stared at it suspiciously.

"What is this monstrosity?"

"Water, electrolytes, and ginger." Then he handed over a banana. "You'll benefit from some potassium, too."

"Are you serious? I thought you were gonna make me a mimosa or something."

He shook his head. "I may be a bartender, but I know fighting a hangover with more alcohol is the worst remedy imaginable. Your gut will thank me later."

I gave it a sip and then chugged, having deemed it drinkable.

Not bad.

I sat the glass down and pressed him for some details.

"What happened last night?"

"Well, you made some new friends…" He washed a glass and gave me a smart-ass look.

Some vague memories returned, such as joining a group of young Galvestonians who were out to paint the town red. Maybe if I found these people, they could tell me what had happened.

"Oh yes, my friends! What a great night we had!" I plastered on a smile.

Jordan grinned, shaking his head. "You don't remember a thing, do you?"

"No, I don't," I said with an even wider smile.

"Well, I'm sorry to inform you that I don't think you and your friends are friends any longer."

"Jesus. What happened?"

"One fella tried to grope you, so you threw a drink right in his face."

I tilted my head, thinking it over. "Well, that sounds reasonable."

"Then you took another drink and threw it in his friend's face."

"Oh. Not so reasonable."

"And then you took another drink and threw it in his friend's girlfriend's face."

I scrubbed my forehead hard, reminding myself that as far as drunks went, I was nothing if not an overachiever. "No signs of intelligent life…." I droned.

Jordan's smug look returned. "And it wasn't even your drink or their drink. It was the drink of another guy who had nothing to do with it at all."

I began to wonder if retracing last night's steps was wise. Perhaps amnesia should be celebrated, beckoned and invited to stay. I swatted at a buzzing fly, annoyed by it and the lack of a refreshing coastal breeze. I needed to get outside and breathe in some humid sea air.

"What did he do?"

"He complained to you. So you took another drink and threw it in his face."

"Where the hell did all those drinks come from? And why the hell did no one stop me?"

I was shifting blame here, but it all sounded a lot like me. I was a famous drink thrower when drunk and renowned for my drawing speed and exceptional aim.

"I'm so sorry," I said, feeling sheepish.

"Oh, don't worry about it. It's fine. They all kind of deserved it."

He winked at me, and I felt slightly mollified. I mean, as long as they deserved it….

"I see you found the tattoo parlor you were looking for." He pointed to my shoulder.

My initial response was to tug down my cap sleeve, but I was trying to get some answers here.

*Ah, fuck it!*

"Are you telling me that before I left, I was actually *looking* to get inked?" I pulled the sleeve up higher and turned toward him, giving him a better view of the odd mess.

He stared at it in disbelief, taking the whole thing in for a moment. "That is a perfect example of what I call drunken regret."

"Yeah, well, this drunken regret is now immortalized upon my damn shoulder. Any chance you know some reason I'd get a spade, and only a spade on my shoulder?"

He shook his head. "Nope."

"And what are those odd lines radiating out from it? Shouldn't they form something?"

"I have no idea what any of that means, but good luck with this aftermath. But if you decide to have it removed, at least take a picture of it for posterity."

"Har har." I probably had taken pictures of something concerning this tattoo. Too bad someone had deleted the evidence.

I left the bar and headed to the front desk, figuring I had a possible shot at getting some intel but knowing it was a long shot at best.

"Excuse me," I said, trying to get the clerk's attention. It was the same guy who had checked me in the day before. I spied his name tag and went with a more casual approach. "Hi, Troy. Great to see you again."

My friendliness did nothing to crack his professional reserve. "Yes, ma'am, how can I help you?"

*Here goes nothing!*

"Is there a snowball's chance in hell of seeing your security footage of me entering the hotel and my hotel room last night?"

The clerk's smile froze as he processed my request. He cleared his throat, clearly not prepared for such an unorthodox question.

"I...uh...I'm afraid that would be impossible. Confidentiality and whatnot. We have privacy laws to consider."

"But it's just *my* privacy we're talking about. No reason for me to be banned from seeing it."

"But...why would you need to see that?"

He made a fair point. Because I wasn't ready to admit to a total stranger that I had been blackout drunk to avoid the overwhelming sense of failure threatening to smother me, I smiled at him and headed to the elevator.

In my room, I changed into my swimsuit and a light blue beach wrap and grabbed a cup of coffee. I put on some sunglasses and headed to the pool, determined to do as my mother had requested. Take a small break, soak up some sun...and plot my next move.

The mystery of this tattoo and how I'd come to have it was not something I intended to chalk up to bad choices while drunk.

I couldn't.

Otherwise, I'd finally have to admit that maybe my father was right. I truly had become just like my mother.

Sip by sip, I continued to replay the very limited events I actually recalled from last night's shenanigans, but I was getting nowhere fast.

As I lounged on my poolside chair, wondering if maybe my next move was to simply visit every tattoo parlor in Galveston, a shadow hovered over me, blocking out the warmth of the sun.

I looked up and then did a double-take. My heart sped up and fluttered erratically as the one man I never thought I would *ever* have to speak to again took a seat on the lounge chair right next to me.

"Miles Westbrook?" I sputtered in disbelief.

"Nice to see you again, Harper."

*Motherfucker!*

# CHAPTER FIVE
## HARPER

"THAT'S QUITE THE ICEBREAKER," Westbrook said while my insides turned to acid. "You always open up a conversation with expletives?"

*Shit. I'd said that out loud?*

But of course I had. This guy had been the source of my torment for months during my investigation of his family. Not to mention the fact that he'd killed my informant and almost killed me. And he had the nerve to approach me like we were old high school buddies?

True signs of a psychopath.

Westbrook seriously scared the shit out of me. We'd had a fun little sit down right before my informant died, and his threats had been less than subtle. I looked around. Several adults lounged poolside, only a few swimming. I wanted to get as far away from this murdering asshole as possible, but I was probably safer sitting here surrounded by several witnesses.

I realized he expected a response from me. Something civil.

"You killed Nora, you goddamn asshole." My throat closed up, fear pounding a chant in my head.

Yeah. That worked.

*Run. Run. Run!!!!*

He looked around, no doubt worried that I had said it too loud.

Leaning forward, he held my gaze and grabbed my arm. Fear shot through me, but I didn't whimper…or piss myself. Pleasant plus.

His gaze was steady as he said in a low voice, "I swear on my life, that was not me, but I did beg you to stop. Don't you remember what I said?"

I ripped my arm from his grip. "I remember everything you said. You threatened to kill me—"

"And that's where I'm gonna stop you because if you had taken the time to understand exactly what I was saying, you would have realized I did not threaten. I warned. I know what my family is capable of, and I was warning you that you had to back off. I had no control over the consequences if you didn't, but you shoved that warning in my face when I had taken a massive risk to meet with you that day."

He sounded convincing, but I had to remember he lied for a living. "You sent me death threats."

He shook his head. "My family sent those."

How convenient. "Your family as a collective whole? Or was there someone in particular?" He paused for a moment, but nothing else was forthcoming, so I pressed on. "I suppose your family also sent someone to drug me and mess with my brakes?"

"Correct."

He looked at me like I was the biggest idiot on the planet for not putting two and two together by now. I looked at him like he was the biggest asshat for suggesting that he wasn't just as guilty as they were.

"And it was your family—not you—that got me fired as well?"

He hesitated, and I saw red.

Before I consciously made the choice, my fist was already headed toward his pretty square jaw, but Miles had impressive reflexes. His hand caught it before I could connect…like it was nothing. As if the slap of my knuckles against his palm didn't sting even a little.

It was a bit insulting, honestly.

But instead of pushing me away, he adjusted his hold, moving his fingers to grasp my wrist and pull me closer, making sure his eyes were level with mine.

"Harper, I swear to God I did it to protect you. You just wouldn't stop, and my family doesn't take kindly to anyone interfering in their affairs."

I stared at him, taking in his micro-expressions, noting his sincerity. The heat from his hand sliding down my arm was distracting and pleasant in a very unpleasant kind of way.

I didn't believe him for one second, but approaching me like this and trying to convince me of his innocence meant he had an angle. I wanted more than anything to find out what that might be.

So here I was…facing my would-be executioner head-on.

For my informant, Nora.

I leaned back a bit.

Miles Westbrook was an intense bastard. Always had been. And I did not like getting "Westbrooked" as so many of my high school friends had. Charming. Handsome. The guy at school that every single girl wanted, and not a single girl seemed able to get.

Not long-term, anyway.

So I was not affected by him or his tanned chest, his board shorts, biceps for days…

At all.

Nope.

He put up a good front, but this motherfucker was rotten to the core.

Still, I was willing to play ball because the way I saw it, I now had an opening to continue doing what I couldn't over a year ago. And this time, Westbrook and his entire family would pay.

"Fine," I said, gentling my tone a bit. I leaned back all the way in my chair. It left me feeling vulnerable, but it sent a message of trust that he needed to believe if I wanted to get anywhere with him. "It doesn't change the fact that I'm now reduced to reporting on sandcastle competitions."

He stared at me for a moment, taking in my body in a way that surprised me because it certainly wasn't the detached move of a killer. It was more like a hot-blooded male showing some definite interest.

And maybe I could use that to my advantage. I'd still have to play hardball and be an utter ass to him, as I had always been. Otherwise, he would be all kinds of suspicious.

After a few more moments, I waved my hand in front of his face.

"Earth to Miles. Are you still with me?"

"You look good," he said suddenly.

WTF?

## MILES

*You look good?*

God, what a stupid response. But seeing her laying there, hair askew, sunglasses perched on her nose, and that anger line on her forehead—one I had come to know all too well—I couldn't help but stumble over my words a little. It didn't help that she was dressed in a two-piece swimsuit that showed a generous amount of northern, white-girl skin.

"I gotta be honest, Miles. That was not the response I expected after blaming you for my current career path. Groveling would have been better."

"Huh?" I asked, feeling a bit dazed.

She sighed like her ability to suffer fools had reached its utmost limit. "I'm reporting on a sandcastle competition here and blaming you for that. The least you could do is pretend to feel sorry about it since it's completely your fault."

"Sandcastle competitions?" Damn her long, dancer legs. I was struggling to keep up here, and that never happened to me.

*Get it together.*

I never heard about such wholesome events and especially never heard of this one. A family of five who could afford to stay at the Seabrook would either leave the kids at home or stay somewhere a little more family-friendly like the Motel 6. I looked around the pool area.

Not a kid in sight.

"It's not a big competition," she said. "But that's all I get now. Little shit. Since someone told my editor to take me off the Westbrook case."

"I'm not apologizing for saving your life. A little gratitude would be appropriate."

Her eyes flared. Oh, she did not like that.

"Gratitude? I was fired, not just taken off the story. Do you get that? And it was all I could do to get this shitty gig. My reputation is trashed, my career is in the toilet, and you—you're walking around like you own the place."

"As a matter of fact, I do." *Kinda,* I didn't add. *And only for now.*

"Fine. You apologized. Said you were sorry. Cleared everything right up for me. Now, why don't you just go fuck some bimbo waitress and leave me the hell alone? Or were you here for something else?"

Chatting with Harper like this reminded me of how very charming she could be.

"Harper, I'm truly sorry. I just needed to see what you were doing here. Make sure you weren't still—"

*Make sure she is not still what?* I asked myself. *Why would my handler say I needed to find her if all she was doing was reporting on some kids playing in the sand for prizes?*

"Investigating your family? Trying to put you in jail? If I had a chance in hell of publishing that story? Because if I had a shred of irrefutable proof, I'd do that in a hot minute." Her scowl deepened if that was even possible, but I could see how she'd be considered beautiful.

"Look, I can't make any of this up to you when it comes to your career, and for that I really am sorry, but maybe I can do something for you."

"Do something for me?"

"I heard you wanted to look at some video footage."

"I do. But that guy at the front desk wouldn't let me."

"I can make them let you. Why do you want to see it, though?"

She put her head in her hands, and I gulped. If it weren't for that cryptic message, I might have left her alone or even worked to tick her off and get her to leave before something bad happened to her. But for some reason, my contact said I needed to find her.

Which meant I needed to make friends. And she was right about one thing, I had very little to offer and no leverage at all.

"I can't believe I am even talking to you. It's only because you own the place, and that maybe you can help me. I'm trying to piece together the events of last night."

"You don't remember them?" I glanced at the table on the other side of her. "Ah, that's why the hangover cure." I motioned to the drink sitting beside her. Jordan had made me the same drink on more than one occasion, and it was easily recognizable. "What's your poison? Tequila?"

I let her think I was some kind of psychic and not that I'd seen exactly what she'd been drinking the night before and who she'd been with.

"How'd you know?" Her eyes narrowed in suspicion, and I knew I was on shaky ground.

"Your eyes simply say margarita." Corny. Bullshit. But better she bought that than me having to tell her the truth.

Harper snorted. "Yeah, right. Okay, Mr. Smarty Pants. If you can tell my drink of choice, then tell me, where did this come from?" She turned her shoulder toward me.

I laughed out loud and then stopped myself. Maybe it was not such a great idea. Her shoulder was decorated with a tattoo, an odd spade in the middle. Maybe I'd been inspired by playing cards, but the central image was surrounded by lines that looked like they should form shapes of some sort. At best, it was strange, and at worst it was incomplete and terrible. The area around the tattoo was red and inflamed, extending beyond where the ink covered.

"That's terrible," I said out loud. "And it looks infected. Even if I could understand what it was supposed to be, the meaning would be unreadable."

"Tell me about it. It stings like a bitch."

I saw her look at me then. Her eyes were traveling up and down my body, and I glanced down at myself, remembering I was only wearing a pair of swim trunks and flip-flops. A bit of a change from the suit yesterday, and not the way she'd ever seen me dressed before.

*Was she checking me out?*

"Where did you get it, anyway?" I asked.

"If I knew that, or anything else that happened last night, I wouldn't need to see the footage now, would I, asshole?"

"My name is Miles, and if you want to see the footage, you'll drop your latest nickname for me."

I watched as her face twisted, whether in pain from the hangover or the very idea of allowing me to help her, no matter how desperately she needed it.

She grabbed her hangover cure and drained it almost to the bottom, belched in a not-cute or ladylike way, and stared at the remainder of the contents.

Then she threw it in my face. The ginger stung my eyes, and I blinked as sticky seltzer water ran down my cheek.

When my eyes cleared, I saw she'd slipped on her swimsuit cover-up and was standing already, grinning at me.

"Yeah, I'd love to see it. Let's go, motherfucker."

Despite myself, I smiled. Why the hell did her aggressive behavior around me always make me feel like I was chasing something I could never have? Especially when I didn't want it. Or her.

"Follow me."

I wanted to know what happened to her last night, too, after I left the bar. That was all. Because maybe I would see some clue about what happened to my FBI contact. Since his cryptic text of "Find Harper Quinn," I hadn't heard a thing.

♠

We approached the front desk, and I saw Troy, our head of customer operations, talking to Ed, the doorman. Ed knew, well, everything that went on here. He must have been early for his shift.

"Hey, you two," I said as I approached.

"Good morning, Mr. Westbrook. Miss Quinn." Ed was tall and thin, dressed in a tailored black suit, light blue shirt, and Mickey Mouse tie. His ice-blue eyes took in everything, and in my experience, he had the memory of an elephant.

"You remember me?" she asked. "I barely remember seeing you when I came to check in yesterday."

"Um, ma'am, forgive me, but you made quite an impression later in the evening," Ed spoke with a formal but fluid manner and a slight accent, South African, if I remembered correctly.

"I did?" she said, looking from him to Troy, who was grinning from behind a tightly trimmed goatee. He was one of the few employees with facial hair, but it suited him well.

"You even asked me out," Ed told her. "You asked me if we could go get matching tattoos."

"You did, ma'am," Troy said. "And you got quite angry when Ed refused."

"Then where did I go?" She looked stunned at this point. This wasn't an act. She really didn't remember a thing.

"I assume you went with your friends and got a tattoo."

"My friends?"

"A group of women you were with. You were laughing and seemed to be having a good time, so I made that assumption." Ed cocked his head, his smile gone, puzzlement on his face. "You really don't remember?"

Harper's shoulders sagged, and she flinched, like that very motion brought her pain.

"Look, Troy, Christopher told Harper here that she couldn't look at the footage from last night, but I'd like to let her. Do you remember about what time she left the hotel, Ed?"

"You aren't letting her look at anything." My sister's shrill tone was like the screech of a needle on vinyl. Goddam Reanne. Showed up at the worst possible time, her usual M.O.

"Hey," I turned. "This is a special situation—"

Reanne looked from me, still shirtless, to Harper, cover up over a swimsuit, wearing similar flip flops, and scowled. "I bet it is."

"It's not what you think. Reanne, this is Harper—"

"I know who the fuck this is," she said. "I just never thought I would see her again, especially with you. What is she doing here?"

I glanced at Harper. Uh-oh. Good thing she didn't have a drink to throw anymore, but I was more concerned that things would come to blows if I didn't step in.

"Hey! Let's just all take a breath." The temperature around me rose. Well, I tried.

"Reanne." Harper practically spat the word at my sister, like one of those velociraptor things in Jurassic Park. It felt like those hideous wing things might sprout from Harper's back any second. "I might ask you the same question. I'm surprised you're not in prison yet."

"I'm surprised you're still alive."

Harper recoiled at that, and I saw fear on her face, not for the first time. I realized it wasn't that she didn't fear our family, or she didn't know the danger. She'd done what she did anyway and had been lucky to survive.

Now that Reanne knew she was here, I had to figure out what my contact thought I needed her for, and get her out of here. Fast.

Her face recovered quickly. "Probably no thanks to you. But I do thank you for the confession that you had something to do with my near accident."

"You mean your drunk driving conviction?" Reanne asked.

"I was never convicted. Unlike you, who will be soon. You're going to mess up, and the FBI is on to you."

*Did Harper know?*

Maybe she knew what I was doing. Maybe the kid castle thing and all of her anger was a front.

"Can I talk to you, Miles?" Reanne asked.

"Not right now," I told her. "I am with a guest, as you can see."

"Fine. But I'm keeping an eye on you." She spun and walked away, but I bet she would not be far.

I turned back to Harper. She just stared.

"Look, Reanne and I are not on the same side," I told her. "We really aren't."

"Coulda fooled me," she said. "But I'm gonna need to see that footage now. Then, once I figure out what the hell happened, I'll get out of here and out of your life."

I tried offering her a smile, but it felt thin, even to me. No chance I was letting her leave before I figured out what my handler meant.

"Let's go then."

I put my hand on the small of her back and steered her toward the security office. To my surprise, she didn't immediately pull away.

*Damn. It's bad enough that I need her,* I thought. *Best not to start caring about her, too.*

*Too late,* came the unbidden thought.

# CHAPTER SIX
## HARPER

AS I APPROACHED the security room alongside Westbrook, I finally understood what it meant to have an out-of-body experience. Never in a million years would I have pictured myself doing anything with this man, willingly or otherwise. Yet here I was, going along with this utter insanity in an attempt to outwit a dude who played the game of life better than anyone I had ever encountered.

But I had little choice. As far as rock bottom went, I'd already hit that a year ago. Yesterday's events had merely added insult to injury. So seriously, what the hell did I have to lose?

Other than my life.

Unfortunately, my impressive grudge holding and deep-seated need for justice—not to mention sweet revenge—meant that I willingly toed that line between life and death like a cat with nine lives.

Last night's few fragmented memories felt fuzzy at best. I couldn't have brought them into focus even if I'd tried.

And boy had I.

But there was one thing that truly bothered me about the total lack of memories. Well, two things, really.

I had never, ever been so drunk as to not remember a damn thing.

I had never had someone delete all of my photos, ensuring I didn't remember a damn thing.

The queasy churn in my stomach was as much from a terrible sense of foreboding as it was from the hangover.

Miles punched in a code on the keypad beside the door. His face was unreadable, but the tension in his jaw suggested he was just as apprehensive about what we might discover.

Which was weird as fuck. What pony did he have in this race?

"We'll start with the footage from the bar and track your movements from there," he said, his voice neutral as he led me inside the dimly lit room.

I eyed him warily, doing my best to *not* look at his massive frame. Nice of him to put a shirt back on. At this point, I was willing to admit that a good chunk of why I'd hated him in high school had everything to do with the fact that he was so damn gorgeous and knew it.

There. I could be honest with myself from time to time.

The security room was a stark contrast to the opulent decor of the Seagate. Monitors lined one wall, each split into quadrants displaying different parts of the hotel. Miles sat at the control desk, his fingers deftly moving over the keyboard as he pulled up the relevant footage.

"Here." He pointed to a screen showing the hotel bar from the night before. "Let's see what we can find."

The footage started innocuously enough, showing me laughing and slightly unsteady,. I had a glass of something in my hand as I mingled with other patrons at the hotel bar. The timestamp in the corner ticked away as scenes of casual revelry continued. I watched, detached, noting how carefree I appeared, oblivious to the storm that was brewing.

But as the minutes ticked by, my on-screen behavior grew increasingly erratic. I was talking animatedly, gesturing wildly, my laughter too loud even through the silent footage. I seriously looked psychotic, and I'd seen enough video footage of me drunk to know the behavior I was exhibiting wasn't normal.

Miles paused the video and glanced at me. "Do you remember any of this?"

I shook my head, frustration gnawing at me. "It's all a blur. Can you rewind the footage to about fifteen minutes before?"

He looked at me quizzically, but didn't argue.

I took a seat next to him to get a better look as he hit play and we watched the events unfold again. Just as we neared the moments where my behavior slowly became worse, Miles paused the video, pointing to a figure at the bar's edge. "Notice anyone unusual?"

I leaned in, squinting at the shadowy outline of a man, distant yet distinctly out of place. "He doesn't look familiar, but something about him seems…off."

"That's because he's staring at you."

A slight chill skipped its way along my spine. "I think he is just looking in my direction."

"I don't."

I didn't either.

We watched for a few more moments, and then the figure moved. His movements were meant to blend in, but they didn't match the intensity on his face. He managed to walk behind me and lightly graze my shoulder with his.

"Did you see that? He touched me."

Westbrook didn't look happy. "I saw it, but I'm not sure what it means. Let's see where you went after this." He fast-forwarded the footage.

The camera captured my exit from the bar, a figure trailing a few steps behind—the same man, unremarkable and yet somehow sinister in his ordinariness. But it wasn't him that caught my attention when Miles froze the frame again. It was the figure slipping out just seconds after me, her presence almost ghost like in the peripheral of the camera's eye.

"Who is that?" My voice was a whisper, an icy dread settling over me.

Miles enhanced the image, bringing her into clearer view. "That's my sister."

My heart skipped a beat. Reanne Westbrook's casual cruelty and sharp intellect had always made her a formidable figure. I'd spent most of our school days convinced she was an absolute sociopath, but boy, could she pretend normalcy like no one I'd ever seen.

And if I'd thought I was afraid of Miles, it was nothing compared to my level of fear when it came to his sister.

She was one scary bitch.

The footage shifted to a street camera, showing me staggering out the door with a few laughing friends in tow . What chilled me to the bone was the fact that Reanne was in the frame as Westbrook paused it…right behind me, looking at me like she was ready to finish what she'd started a year ago.

"Westbrook, why would your sister be in the bar last night? And why did she pretend that today was the first time she'd seen me here?" My voice was tight, each word laced with suspicion.

He didn't answer immediately, his eyes fixed on the screen as he searched for any further sign of her. "I don't know, Harper. But knowing Reanne, it wasn't coincidental."

Miles rewound the footage, playing it back to scrutinize every passerby at the front of the hotel. Reanne didn't appear again after showing up behind me at the entrance.

I was so freaked out. I almost decided the mystery of the tattoo would remain so, but then my lack of self-preservation won out.

As usual.

"I don't think my lost memory is a coincidence," I said. "The way that guy brushed past me, my behavior after that, and then he and Reanne watching me as I left the hotel. Going so far as to follow me to the front…and then what? Are they responsible for this? And why?"

I thought back to the man again, and this time something familiar about him tugged at my memory, but I just couldn't place it. Not right now, but I knew I would put it together eventually.

"But what would the end goal be?" Miles stared at the screen in confusion. "And it's not like he got near your drink and drugged it."

"There are other ways to administer drugs…" My thoughts flew in an entirely different direction, taking me back to the day of the accident. The parking garage. My car. The guy that bumped into me. The sharp pain I felt when he did.

Someone had drugged me the day I had my "accident."

I wondered if the guy from the footage was the same guy who nearly got me killed over a year ago. I kept these thoughts to myself, not trusting Miles and certainly not letting on that I had any idea.

I nodded, my mind racing. If Reanne was behind all this, then what was her endgame? Why the tattoo?

Why the hell didn't she kill me last night when I got back to the hotel?

"Can we fast-forward to when I got back?" I asked.

He nodded and switched to a different camera on my floor. He moved through the footage quickly until we saw activity and then slowed it down. The timestamp at the bottom was nearly 3 am.

I wasn't alone as I drunkenly made my way to my hotel room. Instead, I was leaning against a runty-looking kid wearing clothes that were far too large to be anything other than linebacker hand-me-downs.

"Mikey?" I said, so shocked it came out as a screech.

"Who the hell is Mikey?"

I ignored Miles and stared at the screen, watching this poor kid try to wrangle my unruly ass into giving him my hotel key. Once he realized that was useless, he tried to set me down on the floor, but I was dead weight at that point, and I did more of a flop and roll.

Not exactly dignified.

Miles shook his head. "Whatever you got drugged with looks like it almost killed you. I swear you're foaming at the mouth."

"Oh, look who is absolutely hilarious this afternoon."

Mikey finally found my hotel key in my pants pocket and got the door open. Then he had to do an intricate dance that involved dragging me into the room while leaving one foot planted in the doorway so the door wouldn't close.

I winced when a particularly hard tug made my head hit the doorframe. "I'm so fucking glad I was unconscious for all of this."

"Yeah, well, your kid brother doesn't seem to be having a good night."

"He was my Uber driver from the airport to here."

His eyes widened as he looked at the screen again. "I'd say you owe him a very large tip."

Mikey finally dragged me into the room, and the door slammed shut, hiding our view, but in the corner of the screen I saw something move.

"There!"

Miles froze the screen, and we leaned in closer.

We barely made out the facial features of Reanne, the rest of her body cut off by the frame, but her expression gave me the creeps.

"What is she doing?" I asked.

"My guess? Waiting that Uber driver out. I think she planned on getting in once your Mikey left."

He fast-forwarded the footage until Mikey finally opened the door and skedaddled, looking like he'd just woken up.

*Dear Lord! Did I sleep with him?*

I was ready to pass the fuck out.

Again.

The timestamp at the bottom showed the kid had been there until 9:31am. And at that point, Reanne appeared to be long gone.

"She didn't wait it out. Must have thought he was gonna be there for the long haul." He remained silent for a moment, scrutinizing the frozen frame of Mikey attempting to pull up his ill-fitting pants.

"A little young for you, don't you think?"

"I will punch you for real this time."

"Maybe he was just as drunk as you and had to sleep it off."

I didn't want to think about the implications of a toddler in my hotel room, so I opted for denial and compartmentalization and focused on the more pressing question. "And just what do you think she was planning on doing the moment Mikey left, Westbrook?"

I turned to him, waiting for him to acknowledge something, even though he had always defended Reanne to the death when we were in school.

"I think, Harper Quinn, she was planning on killing you in your sleep."

I sucked in a breath.

Oh, sure. He'd told me his family was dangerous. He was saving me from them. He was protecting me from all that he'd been born into, but never once had he ever been willing to simply name names.

"That stupid-ass kid," I said, furious with Mikey. "He could have gotten himself killed. And what the hell was he doing in my room for so long?"

"It's one of the many questions I'd like to ask him."

Westbrook sounded a bit…nah….no way he was jealous.

"What now? We need to figure out next steps here."

As we left the security room, the weight of everything unsaid hung between us. Reanne's fleeting image in the footage was a clue, albeit a small one, but it was enough to confirm my fears. She was orchestrating something sinister, and now I was more involved than ever.

"I'm not letting you out of my sight. Not until we figure out what's going on."

He might have thought that would make me feel better, but he was dead wrong.

Spending any amount of time with a Westbrook was like testing fate, but I was committed to seeing this through. At the end of the day, I wanted answers.

"Fine," I said, "but I gotta go back to my room and change. And I'm starving, so you're feeding me."

His eyes shone with a hint of mischief, adorable enough to be truly irritating.

"I know just the place if you can contact a certain Uber driver."

I gave him a wide smile. "Why yes, yes I can."

# CHAPTER
# SEVEN
## MILES

HARPER SHIFTED from foot to foot, then paced, then stopped, shifting again. Three minutes later, a late-model Honda Civic roared to the curb, clearly devoid of the stock muffler. A vehicle that, despite its young age, had seen better days.

Harper stared, cleared her throat, and then walked over to greet the driver as he stepped out.

I wasn't even sure there was a person wrapped in all that clothing. Just bulky laundry in haphazard motion.

He tilted back his red baseball cap where scruffy, dirty blonde hair stuck out in tufts around the edges. His round face was baby-smooth. I doubted he'd shaved a day in his life.

Our Uber driver was a ten-year-old.

"Mikey." She stated his name with an awkward flatness.

"Harper!" the Uber driver replied. "How are you? Recovered from last night?"

"About last night—" Harper started, but the driver did something I thought wasn't possible and interrupted her.

"Listen," he said, dropping his eyes to the ground. "I need to tell you something."

"About being in my room all night? And leaving my room after nine this morning?"

"You don't remember what happened, do you?" he mumbled.

"Hey," I interrupted. "Can we talk as we drive?"

Harper shook her head, but it was too late. Mikey shuffled in my direction and extended his hand. "I'm Mikey. Pleasedtomeecha!"

I took his offered handshake, which turned out to be firmer than I thought it would be. "I'm Miles Westbrook."

"Yeah, the dude that owns this place and is part of that crime fam…" He trailed off, realizing what he was saying.

I just grinned, and I could feel Harper's fiery stare even without looking over at her.

"Anyway, sure! I'll fill you in as we drive. Where are we going, by the way?"

"The Steakhouse. We have a table in…" I checked my watch. "Fifteen minutes."

"I'll get you there on time. Hop in!"

Harper looked hesitant, like she was facing her personal execution. Probably not wanting to know what had happened in her hotel room, although judging by this child, nothing much. She took the front seat, and I took the back.

Turned out Mikey was not a good driver. The car shook with any acceleration at all. Or braking. Or rapid turning, swerving from lane to lane, or really any motion.

Which there was a lot of.

"So, aside from us spending the night together, what else happened last night?"

"So, nothing happened. I just want to make that clear," Mikey said. Harper's shoulders sagged with relief. "I took you to your room and managed to get you inside. It was no easy task, by the way. You are an uncooperative drunk."

"You are far more chatty than I remember," Harper mumbled,

and then more loudly, "It's odd because I am normally a very cooperative drunk. Too cooperative."

I stifled a laugh. *Timing,* I thought. *Keep yourself under control.*

Besides that, we were about to learn some vital information concerning the evening before, and I didn't want to interrupt the flow of conversation. A hard left sent me leaning against the boundaries of my seat belt, and I decided to pay better attention to the road ahead, as if I could prevent an accident by simply being more aware than our driver.

"Well, you passed out once I got you into your bed, and I didn't feel right leaving you alone. So I stayed for a while, but I musta fallen asleep."

"Did I pay you at least?" A sharp right caused Harper to lean over the center console, but somehow she braced herself on the dash.

"You may not be a cooperative drunk, but you are a generous one."

"Great. Just great. And where the hell did all of those stuffed animals come from? I didn't see any of that in the video footage."

"Stuffed animals? Ohhhhh." Mikey burst out laughing. "You kept talking about fluffy rabbits from the hotel's gift store. I didn't understand it, but right before I left the hotel, I went down to the gift store and asked the manager to help me deliver as many stuffed animals to your room as possible."

"Are you kidding me? You decided to take a drunk at her word? How the hell much did that cost me?"

Mikey shrugged. "I just told them to charge it to the room."

"Dear old daddy foots the bill." Harper let out a wicked chuckle that made no sense to me. Unless she had daddy issues that surpassed my own.

She sobered quickly enough and any joy she may have felt at her father's expense was quickly overshadowed by our situation.

She rubbed her temple and turned to look at me. "One mystery solved. But not really the most pressing issue. Fluffy rabbits aside, we're still facing one big question mark."

"The tattoo," I said.

"Yep." She gingerly touched her shoulder and winced.

I saw the weight of it all on her then as the Honda sped up and swerved. Lost career. Living in her father's shadow. Trying to prove she wasn't what people thought she was and failing in one night of drunken stupidity that ended with no memory and a horrible tattoo.

It sounded all too familiar to me, right up to the drunken night and tattoo part.

"It's okay," Mikey told her. "Tonight's ride is on me."

Harper sighed. "So, I called you last night? Oh, that's right. You gave me your number so we could bypass Uber booking."

"Yeah. You sounded weird, but your friend got on the phone and told me where to pick you up."

"What friend?"

"You're the drunk. How would I know?"

Harper let out a heavy sigh while I stifled yet another laugh. "Where did you take me last night?"

"Asylum Tattoo, over on Seawall. Great spot. The head artist is really cool. She's a generous drunk, too."

We swerved again and took a left I didn't remember being necessary. Even though I'd been on Galveston Island for a long time, this was a new experience.

I felt lost.

"Did you go in with me?" Harper asked.

"Nope. You told me to wait outside, so I did. About an hour and a half later, that head artist, Frankie, she helped you outside and got you into the car. I took you back to your hotel. You passed out on the way."

"And we know the rest. Thanks, Mikey. That really helps."

"Any other questions?"

"Yeah. How fast can you get us to the tattoo parlor?"

"I thought you were hungry," I said, although I was itching to find answers at that place as well.

"Talk to the tattoo artist first. Eat later." She looked over her shoulder, staring at me in amusement as I held on for dear life. "This Frankie has a ton of explaining to do."

She wasn't wrong.

The Honda braked with a squeal. I was thrown forward, and then back into the seat. "Recalculating route," Mikey said.

I tried not to pay attention to the honking behind us or the expletives being launched from the crosswalk in front of us. If we survived long enough to get some answers from Frankie, it'd be a damn miracle.

"So," Mikey said, glancing at Harper once he got us headed in the right direction, "how'd the tattoo turn out?"

"Terrible."

♠

## HARPER

We pulled into the parking lot with what I'd come to recognize as Mikey's signature parking. Not quite between the parking lines, but somehow still touching both lines with his tires…at an angle. The consistency of his inaccurate parking was an impressive feat.

"Here you go," he said. "Let me know where we're going next."

Then he turned the car off and tilted his chair back, pulling his cap over his eyes and folding his arms across his chest.

I looked behind me, but all I got from Westbrook was a large grin and a shrug.

*At least he's easygoing.*

Mikey was snoring before I was out of the car and closing the door behind me.

"I get the feeling that kid lives in his car," Westbrook said.

I was starting to think Mikey had a few issues at home, but I knew better than to meddle.

Westbrook fell in beside me as we approached the glass doors of Asylum Tattoo. The late afternoon air was brisk, and I shivered slightly, more from anticipation than cold. The parlor was tucked away in a quieter part of town, its vibrant neon signs casting colorful reflections onto the wet pavement.

*Mikey took me all the way out here last night?*

I was never drinking tequila again.

Inside, the familiar buzz of tattoo machines hummed through the air, mixed with the faint smell of antiseptic. Framed designs covered the walls, and numerous ink bottles overflowed the shelves, creating an artist's haven.

I liked the vibe, but I was frustrated that the place didn't look familiar. Nothing registered with me.

"What's wrong?" Westbrook asked, placing a hand on my untattooed shoulder.

A good thing, since my other shoulder was more than a little sore.

"I'm just not getting anything from this place. No memories. No flashbacks. Nada."

"Well, we won't give up just yet. Someone has to remember you from last night. You don't forget a tattoo as ugly as that."

I gave him a wan smile, wishing I had followed through with my impulse during prep school to eviscerate him in the school newspaper.

Regrets were no fun.

A young guy with some seriously intricate sleeve tattoos gave us a nod. "Hi, can I help you?"

"We're looking for Frankie," I said, scanning the busy parlor as if I knew what Frankie looked like.

The guy's expression turned uneasy. "Frankie hasn't shown up today, which isn't like her. Called her house, but we didn't get an answer. You guys family or something?"

The fact that he didn't recognize me was interesting.

*Was he not here last night?*

"Cousin," I said, in case that encouraged the guy to share more information. "She promised me a his and hers tattoo job. Family discount, too." I grabbed Westbrook's arm and held tight, trying really hard not to notice the way his biceps flexed underneath my grip.

The guy smiled. "Sounds like Frankie. Generous to a fault." He rubbed his buzzed head and shrugged. "I don't know what to tell you, though."

"Do you know if she left any messages? She knew we were driving in today, so maybe she left a note."

He shook his head, brow furrowed with worry. "Nothing. It's like she just vanished. But you can check her station if you want. Maybe you'll find something we missed." He gestured to a nicely organized section near the back.

With a nod of thanks, I headed over while Miles stayed behind and engaged the guy in a discussion about the pros and cons of traditional vs. modern tattoo styles. The artist's opinion seemed to lean more toward traditional ink, while Miles took a surprising stance for more modern pieces. I'd never seen a tattoo on his body, even though I had examined much of it far too closely. I wondered if he had one and where he had it hidden.

A small, very naughty part of me couldn't wait to find out until I told myself that I was an insane person and Westbrook was a criminal.

Perfect. Pep talk achieved.

I gave Frankie's workstation a once-over but didn't really notice anything of significance. I turned my attention to her sketchbooks. They lined the shelves against the wall, but there was one that looked a bit out of place. Like it had been put back but only halfway, the owner not having had enough time to finish the job properly.

I grabbed it and flipped through the pages, stopping abruptly when I found a design almost identical to the tattoo on my shoulder. Below it, the words "special projects" were scribbled hastily. There was a page behind the top one, and that looked like a complete tattoo, as if part of mine was missing. I shoved the sketchpad inside my jacket and held it tight against my body, making sure it wasn't at all noticeable.

"We should get going," I said, heading back to what had become an interesting discussion.

"I think you're crazy," the guy said. "Get a tattoo with your mom's initials instead. Relationships are fleeting, but the love of a mom never dies."

My eyebrows hit my hairline. "Interested in tattooing someone's initials on your forehead?" I asked in a sickly sweet tone.

Westbrook chuckled. "I told him about our his and hers tattoos, and he seems to think that tattooing each other's initials on our backs amid decorative floral patterns is an unwise move."

I gave the artist my pearly whites. "But this guy and I are forever." I grabbed Miles by the hand and pulled him toward the door. "Thank you for the help. We'll just head over to Frankie's house and see what's happening. She still lives on Avenue O and 7th, right?"

"Hell no. She moved outta that dump and into that new place on Avenue K, down from Kemper Park. Been there forever. How the hell long has it been since you've seen Frankie?"

"Far too long."

We left in a hurry, heading back to Mikey's car. But just as we reached it, I jerked on Westbrook's arm and halted his momentum. He turned to face me, a question in his eyes.

"Why are you really helping me, Miles? What aren't you telling me?"

He met my stare, nothing but concern glinting from his eyes. "I need to make sure you're safe, Harper. That's all you need to know right now."

"Bullshit. This isn't about my safety."

"The hell it isn't." Now his hand was gripping me, pulling me closer. "You keep thinking the worst of me, Harper. You always have. Ever since prep school. But I have done everything I can to keep you away from my family and safe from the fallout of their choices."

That threw me for a loop. "I don't need protecting."

"You do." He stared at me, his eyes scanning over my face as if noting details he hadn't had the chance to catalog before.

Heat started at the base of my neck, traveling to the top of my head and then skipping along the nerve endings in my arms and legs.

"I don't need anything or anyone."

"I beg to differ. In this situation, you're a damn hazard to yourself, Harper, and you never know when to just let things go. You won't be getting yourself killed on my watch."

Considering I had spent the last eighteen months assuming *he* would be the one to get me killed, this dramatic turn from nemesis to ally left me feeling completely off-kilter.

"Seriously, Westbrook. What's your angle? Let's say I buy what you're selling, and you're really trying to make sure I stay alive… there are easier ways to accomplish that. Like kicking me out of your hotel. Why are you now my chaperone? And why now?"

"I told you. I'm sticking by your side until we figure out the tattoo thing and—"

"Why?"

He stared at me, meeting my gaze in a way that most men couldn't. I felt some grudging respect for the guy, which just pissed me off.

"I'll let you know once I know."

"What the hell is that supposed to mean?"

He let go and jumped in the back seat of the car, slamming the door and making Mikey jolt in the process.

His evasiveness frustrated me, but I couldn't force anything out of him right now. I knew enough about people and personalities to understand that pressing him was a fool's errand. And I was so damn hangry, I wasn't exactly thinking straight either.

I got in the car and directed Mikey back to the Steakhouse. If Westbrook wanted to stay by my side, then I was happy to let him buy me enormous meals of the five-star variety. Five heart-stopping minutes later, we parked, Mikey style, and took a treasured moment to celebrate the fact that not a single one of us had perished in the process.

"You should join us," Westbrook suggested, scrutinizing Mikey. "You look like you haven't eaten in days."

The kid's face brightened at the invitation, and I felt myself thaw a little. Maybe towards Westbrook. Maybe towards Mikey. Which wasn't good. I couldn't afford to care about either of them. But I had a sinking feeling that caring too much was simply an inevitable part of *my* personality.

"They got any good drinks here?"

I rolled my eyes. "Not for you, kid. You're driving. A virgin Piña Colada is in your near future."

Mikey turned to me with a genuine smile on his face, the first one I had ever seen on him. "You sound like a version of my late mom. A super cool one."

*Well, shit!*

# CHAPTER EIGHT
## MILES

"MR. WESTBROOK!" The round man at the podium greeted me.

I should have known his name but didn't recall it. Jeff? Steve?

"And you are?" He gave Harper a pointed look.

The host wore tiny, gold-rimmed glasses as if he were channeling Penguin from the Batman comics. He was short, so maybe the Danny Devito version from the movies.

"This is Harper, my…er…friend." That earned me a scowl, but I had no idea what else to call her. Was she my friend? Companion? Certainly not partner.

*Why did things have to be so complicated?*

"Nice to meet you. I'm Albert!" he said.

*Albert! That was it!*

Harper shook his offered hand. She smiled, but it never reached her eyes. There was a sparkle there, waiting to emerge, but I had yet to bring it out.

Hell, the walking clothes hamper Mikey, got a better reception than I did. But why did I care? My mission was simply to help her recreate the events of the previous night, figure out why my contact wanted me to find her, and then get her out of here before she got herself killed.

So what if she was attractive, passionate, and, if I had to confess to myself, a little fun? She hated me and my entire family. Did I seriously believe I could convince her I was truly on her side? I'd have a better chance of teaching Mikey to drive.

"Your usual table, Mr. Westbrook?" Albert interrupted my thoughts.

"Yes, please." I glanced at Harper and saw that despite herself, she seemed impressed with the place. "And that Bordeaux '76 I had last time, if there is still some in the cellar."

"Do you have good tequila here as well?" Harper asked as we walked past maroon, linen-topped tables toward a smaller one next to the window."

"We do," Albert said, a slight tremor in his voice. He pulled out Harper's chair, and she sat, looking back at him with a smile.

Mikey helped himself to the chair next to her, leaving me the honor of sitting across from the unusual pair.

Albert bowed. "Your server will be right with you."

"Who is it tonight?" I asked.

"Luke," he said, his smile widening.

"Thank you." Luke. My favorite waiter. He stood six-foot-three, managed quite flattering makeup, even in the uniform of the restaurant, and often wore heels, making him appear even taller.

He was a rarity in Texas, a spectacle and institution in Galveston. Not to mention absolutely delightful and punctual in his duties.

I couldn't wait for Harper and Mikey to meet him.

Just as I thought the words, Luke bounced over to us. This week his head was almost shaved, a tiny strip spiked in the center like a miniature mohawk. "Good evening, Miles!" He waved his hands in a "come here" gesture, and I stood and allowed him to hug me.

"And who is this delight?" he asked.

"This is my friend, Harper."

"Oh, a friend, eh?" Luke winked, and his lash extensions brushed his cheek. "You know if you ever want to switch teams, there's certainly a place for you."

"Thanks, Luke, as always, for the offer. Did Albert tell you about the Bordeaux?"

"Yes. And the tequila, miss," he said, turning to Harper and looking her up and down. "When you tire of his boring old wine, let me know, and I'll bring you a real drink."

Harper smiled up at him. "Thank you. I'm pretty sure I'll need it before the evening is over."

The gleam in her eye was certainly not one of passion. She looked angry. Determined. A combo of both.

"And to what do I owe this rare pleasure?" Luke said, turning to Mikey.

"Hiya, Luke. The new lashes are looking good, man."

My eyes widened in surprise, but nothing beat Harper's expression.

"Do you know everyone on this island, kid?" Mikey gave her a quick nod, and she snorted.

"I'll leave you with the menu for a few," Luke said. "You want some water in the meantime? Kid, no booze for you."

"I am of legal age." Mikey straightened up in his chair, but it did him no good.

"Prove it." I waited, but he couldn't produce any ID.

Luke let out a low chuckle as he went in search of beverages.

I turned back to see Harper staring right at me.

"So," she said, crouched and ready to pounce. "Tell me all about you, your criminal activities, your sister, and why she wants to kill me and you don't."

"Uhhhh, not in front of Mikey."

"Oh, don't you worry about me," he said, grabbing a menu. "I ain't no snitch, and I easily forget important, sensitive information of the illegal variety."

"You see? He's fine." She waved at him like he was an errant fly and then lifted his menu higher to block all of him, which wasn't hard to do.

"Don't you want to start with the tattoo and the next steps to figuring out how you got it, why you got it, and then go from there?"

"Oh yeah. We'll get there. But I think I need some background first."

I sighed. This wasn't at all what I had in mind for the evening. I didn't have any illusions that things would be easy, but Harper jumped right in.

"Okay, ask your questions. I'll answer what I can."

Luke showed up with our water. "Ready to order?"

Harper started by ordering a robust meal. I liked a lady who ate more than a salad.

"I'll take the filet on the rare side of medium rare. Keep it bloody but not too bloody. I'll also have a loaded baked potato and a side salad, just to keep things healthy. Get Mikey the same thing, but double it."

I swear to god, the kid made an excited squeal behind the cover of his menu.

I hadn't even seen her look the menu over.

"Your usual, Miles?"

"Not tonight, Luke. I'll have exactly what she's having."

"Of course," he said, scribbling on a tiny pad.

"And Luke?" Harper shrugged off her jacket, clearly ready to get comfortable. I wasn't sure if that was a good sign or an indication that we were gonna be here for a while. "I think I'll start with a margarita after all. Top shelf, the best you got."

"Blended or iced?"

"Blended. And if you see I'm getting empty, refill me."

"Yes, ma'am." Luke spun and pranced away.

"Now, where were we?" Harper pulled out a small tape recorder, set it on the table with the mic between us, and looked at me expectantly.

"You want me to tell you my story while you record it?" I didn't want to get irritated already, but something about her smugness pissed me off. I really wanted to help her, and a part of me wanted to be her friend.

Maybe more. Her and that goddamn smile.

"Yes," she said. "You owe me. My entire life has been upended and nearly ended since I started investigating your family." For a second, I thought her eyes teared up, but she hid it well when Luke arrived with our drinks. She took a giant slurp of her margarita, licking a bit of the salt from the rim of the glass.

"This is really good," she said.

"Good enough you promise not to throw it in my face?" I skated onto thin ice, but it was a delay tactic for sure.

"Funny man. You're buying, so if I have to do any drink tossing, it will just be on your bill. Anyway, you want to prove you are 'on my side'? Then now is your chance."

I looked at the recorder. Why the hell not? I hadn't told anyone my whole story, not even the FBI. I'd have to hold some things back, of course, but maybe if I gave her enough, she would leave part of this the hell alone. Parts that were dangerous for her, that is.

*Who are you kidding? She's in this so deep, and she doesn't even realize it.*

"Fine. I was born in Vegas, not because we lived there, but because mom was at a hotel dad owned on the strip. Vegas was—"

"Jesus Christ!" she interrupted. "If you start that far back, we'll be here all night, and we still have some work to do. Fast-forward." She slammed back the rest of her drink and held her head. "Damn! I never learn."

Luke swooped by, grinning, and her empty glass disappeared.

"You want me to tell you or not?"

She just waved her hand for me to continue while rubbing her temple.

"I had no idea what dad did until I was in Junior High besides being a congressman in Texas. I thought all dads were gone a lot, traveling, and we had money and a nice house. Mom complained from time to time, but not much. I think, in some ways, she was happier when he was away."

"Relatable," Mikey interjected.

"We do not need commentary from the peanut gallery." Harper sipped her drink and nodded for me to continue.

"Around my eighth-grade year, dad was running for reelection…"

"And for the record," she said, pointing at the recorder, "your father is Cameron Westbrook?" She took a long sip from another fresh drink that had somehow appeared in front of her as I talked.

"Yes, that's correct." I let my annoyance show in my voice. "Anyway, he was running for reelection, and there were rumors about illegal activity or mob connections or something. It's all a bit fuzzy. I was young."

"His opponent hit hard, trying to prove he was not a man of the people or a good guy. Our pastor and a bunch of other church leaders stood up for my dad and his integrity. Then his opponent got popped for a DUI."

"Sounds familiar." Harper's voice dripped with sarcasm. "Old habits die hard."

"Maybe. I don't know. Dad won, but the allegations continued to circle, at least in the rumor mill. Reporters would come to the house and ask Mom questions. Sometimes they would ask me, too."

"And what did you and your mom say?"

"We told them we didn't know, and that was the truth, at least for me. But other men would show up to meet with Dad when he was home. Stories would suddenly disappear from the news, and pretty soon, no one was talking that way about him anymore."

"But you suspected?"

"More than suspected. I saw something…that story is for another day."

This time, when Luke moved into the picture, I ordered another old-fashioned. My mind wandered back to getting up to get a drink late one night and seeing two men leaving my father's office carrying a heavy rug. I followed them…

I didn't have time for that reflection. The next day, my dad had a new rug delivered to his office, and I never told him what I saw. I'd never told anyone. Harper would not be the first.

"What did you see?"

"I'm not saying. I had tried sports by then—"

"I remember."

"Yeah. You saw me as a jock, right?"

"You and your stuck-up, rich football buddies. So, yeah."

My offense at her obvious disdain got sidetracked for a moment by Mikey's impressive ability to eat one of his steaks in two bites. He dug into his bounty like it was his last meal for the week.

Once the thought hit me, I worried that might be the case.

Fantastic steak as always. I chased it with the last of my old-fashioned and set the empty glass on the edge of the table.

"Do you know what position I played?" I was happy to see she'd slowed down on her drinking. Maybe she would actually hear me.

Harper looked thoughtful and then shook her head. "Who cares? You guys were all the same."

"I was the kicker."

Mid drink, she laughed, spraying margarita all over her plate and onto the table. She grabbed a napkin and began wiping it up, but her lack of embarrassment was no surprise.

Couldn't take this woman anywhere.

"The kicker? Isn't that kinda like the bass player in a band? Did you even—oh, that is hilarious!"

"Harper, look at me. Really look."

She did, studying my face and my body for a moment. Her eyes moved over my chest and what she could see of my arms under my shirt and then back up to my eyes. I hoped she could see sincerity there, but I also hoped she couldn't read the pain I was feeling at that moment.

"And?" she asked, a bit hoarsely.

"I'm athletic, yes, but I'm too small for most football positions and not fast enough. Jordan, on the other hand, was fast and tall and had it all going for him. But the NFL always needs kickers. It's not glamorous, but it gets you in the league and can make you a good living."

"And you were good enough for the NFL?"

"So was Jordan, but we bonded over similar experiences."

"Like?" she said, a huge bite of loaded potato hovering between her mouth and her plate.

"Jordan got one too many concussions. Knocked him right out of the draft. Me? I blew out my knee in my final game as a senior. Killed my dreams right there."

"So you came to work for your dad?"

"There was family pressure." I took a moment to eat some of my dinner. My stomach growled like my throat had been cut, and besides, I needed something to absorb some alcohol. I needed to be at least a little sober to ride back to the hotel with Mikey.

Or wherever we went after this.

"Then what?"

"I worked. I learned. I saw the inside of the business, how my dad took care of those who crossed him, and how well he treated those who fell in line. I tried to straddle the line of doing the right thing and making him happy."

"How did that work out?"

"It didn't. I saw what happened to Nora. I tried to warn you to stay away. Clearly, that did not work. And that's all I'm going to say tonight."

"So you're not on your dad's side anymore? You're on mine."

I took another bite of steak and chewed thoughtfully. I'd already said too much. I looked around to make sure no other diners were close enough to have overheard.

My nerves tingled. I'd already gone too far.

"Okay. Maybe not mine. Whose side are you on?"

"I just want you to be safe," I told her. "So I can't tell you what happened next. Not right now. Maybe not ever."

"So, your sister?"

"She has always been Dad's favorite."

"What does that mean?"

"It means, as far as I know, she still works closely with him. He is probably why she is here, to check up on me."

"Are there things for her to check on?" Harper stared at me, and I returned her gaze.

"Harper, I am not saying any more tonight."

"Why not?" she pressed, and I wanted to give in so badly. God, her smile was cute, her piercing eyes under those gorgeous curls, her neck, those shoulders…

*Focus, Miles. The fucking tattoo. My contact is missing. My sister is watching my every move, and clearly hates Harper enough to want her dead.*

*Focus.*

*But she is beautiful, and pretty much everything you've wanted since prep school.*

*A pain in the ass, too.*

"Because if I tell you, you will be in even more danger than you are now. We need to figure out your tattoo situation as soon as possible and get you out of Galveston."

"Get me out of here? That's all you want, huh?" Her anger flared. She stuck the last of her potato in her mouth, chewing rapidly. Her steak had disappeared as I talked. A fresh drink sat in front of her.

"Yes!" I said. "You either refuse to or don't understand. Reanne will kill you. My father might want you dead for all I know. If they think you are investigating them again, you won't live through the week. And somehow, some way, they will make it look like an accident, and I—"

I stopped. My eyes watered, and I fought to stop them. "I can't be responsible for another death. Do you understand me? I have a plan, a plan to end all of this once and for all. And you are not a part of it!"

"Read the room, man." Mikey sipped his nonalcoholic beverage, but he appeared to be inching closer to me as Harper's gaze took on a terrifyingly determined glint.

"I do not need your permission to stay or to go. While I appreciate your concern for my well being, I don't believe for one second it's altruistic in nature. You're playing a different game here. And I intend to figure out what that game is, and I don't have to include you in the process."

She stood as Mikey quickly swallowed the rest of his drink and then shoveled the last of his meal in his mouth.

"Fine. You don't want to include me? No problem! I'll go find Frankie myself and get some answers. And then I need to get out of here. Motherfucker!"

Other diners were looking now, staring.

"Harper, just have a seat," I begged now. "I really am trying to help you, and you should not go alone. It's not safe."

"I'll take Mikey. At least I know he isn't trying to kill me."

"Maybe. It's hard to tell from his driving." Wrong moment to lighten the mood, it turned out. Now I was wearing the last of my drink, and a large, round ice cube sat in my lap.

I forgot how prone she was to drink-throwing when alcohol and anger were involved.

"Deeply offended, bro." Mikey patted my shoulder, not appearing even remotely miffed by anything I'd just said.

He knew truth when he heard it.

"Traitor," I muttered.

He grinned wide. "She's a better tipper."

I stood, ice and liquid dripping to the floor. "Fine. You want to go, go. Reanne may be waiting for you right now. And if you think that boy you have driving you around will be any protection at all, best of luck. But I can protect you, and if I can do that for a few more days—"

"A few more days? What happens then?" she shouted.

I looked around. Wide eyes over open mouths surrounded us. This was not the time or place.

"Harper, just come with me, and I'll explain."

"Oh, poor Miles. Did I embarrass you at your fancy-wancy restaurant? Why don't you bite me? Find your own way back to the hotel. I'm leaving."

"It's past ten. You can't go wandering around Galveston by yourself, not in Frankie's neighborhood."

"Who says?"

"Harper!"

But it was no use. I'd lost her. She spun on her heel and stomped away. I wanted, no, needed, to follow her. But I needed to salvage this at least a little.

Luke approached with a shit-eating grin. "That was unexpected, but exciting." His chuckle was damn annoying. "She's feisty!"

"She sure is. Can you put this on my tab? I think I need to go chase her down before she does something stupid."

"Sure, Mr. Westbrook, but can I be honest?"

"Why not?"

"I think you're the one who did something stupid. It's clear you two like each other. My hetero radar says the two of you are destined for each other. Whatever she wants to know, just tell her."

"I would, Luke, if I could."

He studied me for a moment, his interest clearly piqued. "Is it that you can't? Or that you won't?"

I smiled, patted his shoulder, and rushed out of the restaurant. At least I knew where Harper was headed. I just needed to find a taxi driver who could get me to Frankie's before she did.

With the way Mikey drove, I seriously doubted my luck.

# CHAPTER NINE

## HARPER

PULLING up to Frankie's place was like entering Raccoon City from *Resident Evil*. While there were some nice areas in Galveston, I was surprised, and rather alarmed, at the insanity that was Frankie's dwelling.

Overflowing bags of garbage, broken-down cars, and—dear Lord—I stared wide-eyed at an actual raccoon sitting atop the side of an industrial dumpster, chewing the hell out of a feral cat. It was the showdown I never knew I needed.

"I cannot look away," Mikey said. "Bet you ten bucks Raccoon lands a sucker punch before things go south." Mikey came to an abrupt stop and parked the car.

I no longer had to brace for it since I spent the entire ride preparing for the end either way.

"You're on, kid. Never underestimate Garfield when his ribs are showing."

"Uh, are you sure you wanna go in there?" Mikey gestured to Frankie's front door.

Even from here, I saw it was wide open and hanging awkwardly on its hinges. My heart sank.

"Shit."

We got out of the car to the melodious sounds of Raccoon and Cat having it out inside the garbage can. The soundtrack was fitting.

As Mikey and I approached Frankie's quaint bungalow, adrenaline kicked in. The setting sun cast long shadows across the unkempt lawn, and the front door creaked softly as the evening breeze nudged it.

An ominous welcome, indeed.

"I don't like this," Mikey muttered beside me, his usual bravado dampened by the sight.

I nodded, feeling my reporter's instinct kick in over my nerves. I made a motion for him to stay put as I pulled out my phone, using it as a flashlight, and stepped cautiously into the living room. The scene inside spelled chaos: furniture overturned, drawers emptied, and personal items strewn across the floor. Someone had been searching for something—desperately.

My thoughts flashed back to Nora's place and the way I'd found her body. Not a thing had been touched. Nothing out of place. It had all been so perfect. A little too perfect. And then I found Nora on her couch, dead from what the medical examiner would later rule as suicide via an overdose.

Suicide.

I hadn't bought it for one minute.

For some reason, the chaos of this scene made me feel better. If things were awry, they damn well better look like it.

"Someone beat us to it," I whispered, my light sweeping across the wreckage. I turned and headed back out to the porch. "Kid, you're going back to the car."

"What?" he hissed, outrage written all over his face. "I'm not—"

"You are." I grabbed him by both shoulders, alarmed at the bones I felt protruding there. "Mikey, it's one thing to have you tag along and drive me places, but this scenario just got really dangerous. Instead of asking Frankie questions, we've stumbled on an entirely different scene, and I've already lost..." I bit back the name, Nora, before it left my lips. "I don't have the greatest track record when it comes to putting someone else's safety first, and I'm not making the same mistake again. You will get in that car, you will lock the door, and at the first sign of trouble, you will take off without me. Do you understand?"

His stubborn glare told me he read me loud and clear and had no intention of doing a damn thing I'd just said.

Which meant he was a younger version of me.

Karma was quite the bitch.

I met him glare for glare until he shrugged out of my grip and stomped back to the car, giving me one last side-eye before he opened the car door.

"Lock it," I said.

"You know I'm a grown-ass adult, right?"

"You really want me to answer that question, Mikey?"

He rubbed his nose and sniffed before getting in. I didn't move until the door was shut and I heard the locks engage.

The hiss of Raccoon and Cat continued as I turned back and entered the living room again.

I headed down the hall, checking the first open door on my right and recognizing a home office. It was a complete disaster. Every drawer ripped open, some dumped on the floor, their contents strewn about the place.

My flashlight beam landed on a pile of shredded paper in the corner. Kneeling down, I delicately lifted a few intact pieces. Among the fragments, one caught my eye—a piece with a partial FBI letterhead visible.

That did not bode well. What tattoo artist found themselves in need of shredding mail from the FBI?

Before I could examine it further, a noise from the back of the house startled me.

If that kid had disobeyed me, there would be hell to pay, followed by heavy drinking.

I was such an asshole. Didn't matter that this kid drove. He was clearly a minor, and like the self-absorbed reporter I was, the story took front and center, frequently at the expense of others. I'd promised myself to never let another Nora—another informant—or anyone else, for that matter, die on my watch.

And like a selfish idiot, I'd encouraged this kid to enter a house that had already been broken into. Then I sent him out alone in his car in this neighborhood. I should have just hustled us out of the place and told him to drive literally anywhere else but here.

My pulse quickened as I moved toward the sound, out into the hallway, heading to the back and to the left, only to stop dead in my tracks at the sight of a shadowy figure rifling through the kitchen drawers. Without thinking, I ducked back behind the door frame, holding my breath.

The intruder paused, then resumed his search more frantically. I seized the moment to sneak a glance. He was big, dressed in dark clothes, his back to me. A gun tucked into his belt sent a chill down my spine.

Suddenly, a loud thud came from the living room—Mikey. My protective instincts flared. I stepped out and shouted, "Hey!"

The intruder whirled, his face masked, but at the sound of my voice, he bolted for the back door. I chased after him, not thinking about the fact that he had a gun and could have used it on me. Going after him was the stupidest thing in the world to be doing right now, but I couldn't get my legs to stop.

When I ran through the back toward the yard, I saw nothing. Panting, I turned and ran back down the hallway, trying to get to Mikey as fast as I could. The kid was rubbing his head and searching the floor, looking bewildered.

"Are you okay?" I rushed to his side.

"Yeah, I fell over…look at this." He pointed to what had tripped him—a small, locked box partially hidden under a loose floorboard he'd unwittingly dislodged.

I moved the board aside, keeping my eye on the hallway in case the guy came back. I was really kicking myself for letting my temper get the best of me with Westbrook. My pride never failed to bite me in the ass at the worst of times, and having him here as backup would not only have been a smart move, but a necessary one.

I had no weapon, and Mikey and I looked like easy prey.

*Because we are.*

I grabbed the box and Mikey's hand, and then we hauled ass to the car just as headlights swept down the grimy road toward us. I handed Mikey the box and shoved him behind me, ready to take the gunman head-on.

When I realized it was a taxi, I was more than a little confused. It parked just in front of us and out stepped Westbrook, his expression grim.

The relief that suffused me at seeing his handsome face did not make me happy.

"Harper, we need to talk," he called out as he approached, his eyes noting the way I was still strong-arming Mikey into staying behind me. "Did I miss something?"

"What are you doing here?" I demanded, my trust in him hanging by a thread.

"I followed you. I was worried," Westbrook confessed. His gaze fell on the open door behind us. The damage was pretty obvious from here. "And it seems I was right to be."

"Too late, Westbrook," I said, my voice cold. "Frankie's gone, and I just stumbled onto the guy that ransacked her place."

"Did he see your face?"

I nodded, hating having to confirm how reckless I'd been.

Westbrook shook his head and swore. "I lost you for ten minutes and you nearly got yourself killed?"

"But we found something cool under the—"

"Not here, Mikey." I looked around, realizing the neighborhood was way too quiet, Raccoon and Cat having ended their argument and left for parts unknown. The silence hung heavy and menacing, and I did not want anyone to know what

Mikey and I had found. We weren't debriefing Westbrook until we were safe.

"Let's get in the car and get the hell out of here." I turned to Westbrook. "I'll explain everything on the way."

"On the way to where?"

"Anywhere but the Seagate Hotel."

# CHAPTER TEN
## MILES

I HAD the itch to look inside Frankie's house, if you could call it that, but Harper wasn't just scared. She was terrified and probably should be. If she'd actually surprised whoever had been ransacking Frankie's place, if that person were armed, well, they could be back at any time.

And a burglary in this neighborhood made no sense at all. Frankie had to be more than a tattoo artist—no one would come try to rob any house in this neighborhood unless it was a junkie looking for a fix.

Harper hadn't mentioned a body, which made me wonder where Frankie was.

"Let's go!" she tugged at my arm, and I realized Mikey was in the car, waiting. Probably scared to death. Even if I came back and had a look, it would have to be on my own.

And I had to get Harper somewhere safe. She was right not to go back to the Seagate—not after what had happened the last couple of days. But me? I couldn't just disappear from my business with her and some Uber driver without sending up flares and smoke signals everywhere.

Too many people in this town knew who I was.

Not to mention Reanne being here, and the FBI closing in.

Ideally, I would just put her on a plane—

"Westbrook!" Now she held the car door open, and I folded my frame into the back seat, waving away my previous taxi driver. She glanced back at me as Mikey took off before the door even closed. Her eyes were wild, and as she turned to face forward, her head darted back and forth, looking for something—or rather someone.

Mikey took a right, the car barely staying on two wheels, and sped down the boulevard. After a few blocks, he slowed from insanity speed to something slightly over the legal speed limit.

"Where to?" Harper asked, turning back to look at me.

"I know just the place," Mikey said. "At least for now. You guys got any cash?"

"I have a few hundred bucks," I said.

"That will take care of it," Mikey answered. Until this moment, I hadn't noticed the tremor in his voice, but it was there, a boy trying to be brave.

We pulled into a part of Galveston I rarely saw, and swung into what I assumed used to be a parking lot. Some asphalt remained, along with some weeds courageously poking through it, but most of it seemed to be a mix of sand and clay. The place stood on stilts of sort—some of which had been clearly shorn up by fresh framing—new posts clamped to old ones, and some other fixes that looked iffy at best.

The upper part of the structure, reached by questionable stairs, contained a walkway bordered by a wooden rail that had seen better days. A few of the doors were open, box fans set in them moving hot air from outside to the inside, making me wonder what kind of ovens those rooms were.

"Mikey. We can do better," I said. "This is a bit extreme."

"What do you suggest?" Harper said, turning. "Another hotel your father owns? Somewhere they would suspect we would go?"

"Who is they? My family? Who?"

"The guy at Frankie's. He one of yours? Or your father's? Just how far are you willing to go to get me out of here?"

"Harper, I need you." I realized the words I'd just said and wished I could take them back.

She stared at me and opened her mouth to say something.

"We going in, or what?" Mikey asked. "People are staring."

A man, dressed in what could best be described as rags, smiled at us. Three teeth clung desperately to his upper gums.

"Not here, Mikey. There has to be somewhere better."

He sighed. "There is. I just don't want to go there."

"You'd rather be here?"

A woman pushing what once had been a grocery cart approached the front of the car.

"No," he said and reversed out of the parking lot, narrowly missing a third man, this one dressed in tattered shorts, not wearing a shirt, and with a Jesus beard that nearly reached his nipples.

As Mikey took the next corner, the box he'd been holding slid across the seat and hit me on the thigh.

"What's this?" I asked.

"It came from Frankie's," Harper said. "We'll explain when we get...wherever." She had grown strangely silent, and there was a tiredness in her voice. Exhaustion maybe.

I knew the feeling. Adrenaline lasted only so long, and then there was the crash.

We pulled up at another hotel, this one looking much better than the first, although still not a world-class joint. There was actually a parking lot, and there were cars rather than carts parked out front.

A neon sign read "Office" and the No in the No Vacancy sign remained unlit.

"Much better," I said.

"Yes," Harper interjected quietly. "Here at least the biggest danger is a lumpy mattress and the wifi might be pretty weak."

"It's actually nicer than it looks," Mikey said.

They walked into the office, and a tall, thin woman almost my height walked out of the room behind the office.

"How can I help—Mikey! So good to see you!" She came around the counter, arms open for a hug.

"Hi Auntie," Mikey said. "We need a room for a couple of days."

♠

Once we sorted out who Mikey's auntie was, the fact that she wouldn't take our money for a room, and insisted on hugging Harper while she side-eyed me suspiciously, we found ourselves in a room with two queen beds stuffed into the small space, a tiny walkway between them.

A dresser held a television that looked like it came from a discount store, but it worked. Harper turned it on and set the volume high enough to muffle our, and then turned to us. I sat on one bed, Mikey sat on the other still holding the box.

"Okay," she said, barely audible over the television. "Let's open that box."

"Not before you catch me up," I said.

She told me the story of entering Frankie's place, finding it trashed, and then seeing the papers with the FBI logo on the top.

"Then I saw the guy going through some drawers, saw that he had a gun, and I chased him."

"He had a gun, and you chased him?"

"Not the smartest thing. But I couldn't let him get to Mikey."

"And you hit your head when you fell over this box?" I asked the kid.

"Yeah. I kicked a floorboard as I came through the door—"

"Which you were not supposed to do. You were supposed to stay in the car. Doors locked." Harper glared, but Mikey just looked at his hands.

"I couldn't leave you in there alone. I had a bad feeling."

"Mikey...grrrr!" Harper literally growled at him. She looked around the room then. "No fridge. No mini-bar. Probably for the best."

"Okay, okay!" I raised my voice just a little. "So Frankie—the FBI? A tattoo artist? What the hell is going on here?"

"Earlier you said you needed me." Harper sat down next to Mikey and moved the box on the other side of her. She looked into my eyes. "What did you mean by that?"

I sighed. The gig was up, and with Frankie's apparent connection, I knew we needed all the facts on the table in order to figure this out.

So I told her. How I was working for the FBI, trying to bring the Westbrook empire down, and how my contact had been a no-show. I held out my phone so she could see the message.

"Find Harper Quinn." I watched her face as I spoke. Her eyebrows rose and fell, but she didn't say a word until I finished.

"You...you motherfucker!" Her face reddened, her legs crossed and uncrossed as if she wasn't sure what to do with them. "You ruined my life! My career! Supposedly all while trying to protect me. Then your 'contact' tells you to find me?"

"I didn't know you were here. I don't know how he knew you were here, or what you have to do with any of this."

"I didn't choose to come here. I was sent on assignment by my—"

"Your what?"

"My editor." She stood and tried to pace, but it was a short runway, only room for about four steps before she had to turn around. The space between the end of the beds and the dresser could not be called generous. Those long legs made short work of it, and the way she folded her arms and tossed her hair...

*Knock it off, Miles.*

"So you are getting close, but you needed what?"

"My contact had information I needed to get into my father's records, the real ones, so I could copy them. That is the last piece of the puzzle. I've seen them, but they're locked behind a network, and my dad has the password with some kind of added authentication."

"This information can bypass that?"

"It's some kind of code."

"Computer code?" Mikey said. "Like encryption and stuff?"

"Yeah," I said. "Why?"

"Hand me your phone."

I debated about which one to hand him but chose my personal phone over the burner. There was a password and biometrics on it, as well as a new security feature I didn't quite understand. But no password. Without my face, there was no possibility of getting in.

He looked it over and pushed a couple of buttons. Then typed in a code before he handed it back to me.

Open.

"How did you—"

He shrugged. "I learned some stuff along the way."

"So you think you can crack my father's code?"

"I have no idea. But if you find the data you are looking for, I can sure try."

"Mikey, you have hidden talents, my man. What are you doing driving for Uber?"

"Beats being a hotel manager and tied down to this place," he said, and I realized he was teasing me.

"Okay, whatever your reasons, I'd appreciate the help."

"So what will this data you need look like?"

"It's a thumb drive and a code of some sort. Supposedly pretty easy once you know it."

"Do you know where your contact was staying?"

"No. The FBI doesn't exactly share that information with informants."

"So it could be anywhere?"

"Yeah." I shrugged.

"Well, first things first," she said, taking charge. "Let's see if we can pick this lock and get this box—"

I heard a click and turned to look. Mikey sat, grinning, the lid on the box wide open.

"Like this?" he said.

"Motherfucker!" Harper said, this time with some joy in her voice. "Give that to me."

She opened the lid and pulled out a plain manila envelope, and underneath it was a deck of cards.

# CHAPTER ELEVEN
## HARPER

I OPENED the folder and dumped out its contents, frowning as I sifted through the assorted passports and currencies—evidence of Frankie's preparedness to flee at a moment's notice. Each passport displayed a different identity, complete with meticulously crafted aliases and a variety of currencies.

"Whoa," said Westbrook. "Frankie seemed prepared to leave."

"Yeah, and apparently she brought entertainment for the trip." I moved the deck of cards to the side, more interested in the US passport with the name Frankie Jones on it. "You think Frankie is an alias as well?"

"Probably. I don't think this woman has been using her real name for a while now." Westbrook grabbed Mikey's hand just as it moved to swipe a Benjamin from the stash.

I chuckled and looked more closely at the rest of the box's contents.

"Look at this." I picked up a well-worn notebook. The pages were filled with dates, coded messages, and names. Some I recognized as contacts from my old investigative reports. It was as if Frankie had been leading a double life, one that intersected with the very stories I'd chased.

When I saw Nora's name, my throat went dry. I closed it quickly, too spooked by its contents to keep going.

Westbrook stared at me for a moment and then gently took the notebook from my white-knuckled grip. I waited as he studied some of the pages, his eyes getting wider by the second.

"She seems to know a lot more than she should. It's as if she's been following your career."

"More specifically, my progress on the story involving your family."

Beside the notebook, a small digital recorder lay nestled between stacks of euros and yen. I grabbed it, pressed play, and Frankie's voice filled the room, terse and urgent, discussing movements and meetings that didn't make sense without context. "If you're listening to this, things have likely gone south," Frankie's recorded voice said, making my skin itch.

Westbrook and Mikey leaned forward, listening intently as Frankie's voice grew more urgent.

"No sense in looking for me, Conners. If you're listening to this, then that ship has sailed. Just tell the boss that we've got... Quinn."

"Who the hell is Conners?" I asked.

Westbrook made a choked sound. "Conners is the name of my handler. But Frankie also said Quinn. Why are you and Conners being mentioned in this recording at all?"

"Your handler?"

"Part of my story that I can't tell you about right now. Not without putting you in even more danger."

"You're going to elaborate, you motherfu—"

"What was that muffled part before it?" Mikey interrupted.

He grabbed the recording and played it again, but the sound never got better. It hit a patch of static, making it indiscernible.

*What the hell is really going on here?*

"Miles, you need to come clean right now, or I swear—" The ring of my phone caused me to leap off the bed.

"Shit," I said, grabbing at my chest. I checked the number and let out a low growl.

Westbrook's lips quirked. "Not someone you want to chat with?"

"It's my dad," I said. "I need to chat with you, but this can't wait." I answered it, knowing I needed to get this confrontation over with as soon as possible.

"What is it?"

"Jesus, Harper, do you always answer your phone like that?"

"I do when you're on the other end."

I heard a long-suffering sigh. I was not surprised that I had once again disappointed him.

"Look, I have a job for you. I'd like to chat about it over drinks. Your boss said you were at the Seagate."

"Cut the shit. You and I both know you paid my boss to book me there. Which does not at all surprise me. You offering me a job does, though."

"Come on, Harper. I'm not all bad, you know. We used to get along famously."

I swallowed down the bile, not to mention the immense sadness I felt at the fact that this statement might have been true when I was little. Yet the older you get, the easier it is to spot a toxic narcissist, and my dad was as toxic as they came.

"I'll meet you for drinks literally anywhere else but the Seagate. Just text me the address and I'll be there soon." I hung up before he could respond. "Miles, we are not done with this discussion. To be continued."

"I can take you." Mikey stood and grabbed his keys.

Westbrook hadn't moved. Just stared at me with a speculative look on his face. "I see we both have daddy issues."

"Stop trying to find more common ground with me, Westbrook. I'm never gonna like you."

He gave me a smirk, one that oozed with what I considered unfounded confidence. "Interesting thing to deny at the moment,

Harper." I opened my mouth to say more, but he reached over and grabbed my hand, lacing his fingers in mine, effectively shutting me up due to the shock of it. "You're right, though. We do need to talk as soon as we can."

Westbrook is holding my hand? It may or may not have been a long-time fantasy of mine when I had been a lowly freshman, but I was not that little girl any longer.

I stared at him, waiting for…what, I wasn't sure, but he just maintained eye contact, communicating that he saw me.

I didn't like it. Didn't like being seen.

Whatever voodoo spell Westbrook had managed to place me under finally broke with the buzz of my phone. I glanced down to see my dad's text message. Almost simultaneously, Westbrook's phone lit up with a message of his own.

"I have to head back," he said, his frustration evident. "With Reanne snooping around, I can't be seen neglecting my duties or being caught with you guys. Why don't you go meet up with your dad, and we'll rendezvous back here in a couple of hours."

"Sounds like a plan," I said, letting go of his hand with alarming reluctance. "But what do we do with all of Frankie's stuff?"

"I'll give it to my aunt. She's got a safe in the back. No one has any idea we got it back there." Mikey put everything back in the box, locked it up, and raced out, looking like he'd just shoplifted a lunch box from Walmart.

Guilt tore at my insides again. I didn't want him to keep working with us. "We need to keep Mikey out of this."

"He's already in this, Harper. Reanne saw him. He's on video footage. He's been with you every step of the way here. I honestly think he is safer with us than trying to do a side investigation on his own if we cut him loose. You think for a moment he'll leave this be, even if we don't let him drive us around anymore?"

Thinking back on how much Mikey reminded me of me, I let out several expletives.

Westbrook nodded, not needing anything else to confirm that I understood. "Keep him close. I'll see you guys in a couple of hours."

"Fine," I muttered as I watched Westbrook leave the room, catching myself checking him out in the process.

There was something seriously wrong with me.

♠

As Mikey pulled up to The Brick House Tavern, my insides did a double flip and then a nose dive. I didn't know how long I sat there in the parking lot staring at the bar's neon sign until Mikey made a coughing noise to get my attention.

"Just how bad is your pops, Harper? You want me to go in with you?"

The question pulled a smile from me, a miracle with my jumbled emotions. I considered him for a moment, realizing I didn't know much about him. "Tell me about your dad, Mikey."

He gave me a side-eye, and at first, I thought he would ignore the question. He scratched an ear and tugged, appearing nervous for a moment.

"The truth is, I'm a foster kid. I just call Suzie my aunt because it makes me feel connected to her, but I'm one of three kids she fosters because she's a good person. My dad's in prison for dealing. Mom died in a car accident when I was eight."

"Shit, kid. I'm sorry I asked."

He smiled, one that actually reached his eyes. "I'm one of the lucky ones. Aunt Suzie is a good woman, and she keeps us fed, a roof over our heads. It's about all she can do, though. The rest is up to us. Considering who our dads are, Harper, I'm thinking that we're better off without 'em. We're who we are in spite of them."

I gave him a long, hard stare, reassessing Mikey and realizing that wisdom came in all shapes and sizes…not to mention ages.

Out of the mouths of babes…

"Stay safe and out of the way. I don't like you anywhere near my dad or this investigation, so lock the doors and keep your eyes open."

He shook his head and grinned.

"What's so funny?" I asked.

"You just sound like a mom."

"Watch your mouth, kid."

I got out of the car and headed for the entrance, feeling slightly less off kilter.

Upon entering, I spotted my dad in the far corner almost immediately. Hard to miss his slicked back hair and polished appearance. He never went anywhere unless he was dressed to the nines. As I approached, he stood, giving me a smile that seemed genuine, but that was my dad. Beguiling right up until he went for blood.

"How are you, sweetheart?"

I ignored the question, knowing he didn't give a shit either way.

"I'm really not here for drinks or chit chat, Dad. I would like to know why you're here and why you took over my hotel arrangements."

"Harper," he began, his voice low, "I booked you at the Seagate because I thought it would be a good beginning for mending bridges."

"Mending bridges?" My eyes bugged. I could actually feel them trying to leap out of my eye sockets. "These people tried to kill me last year, and you thought we'd all sing kumbaya?"

"Shifting blame for the DUI is beneath you, and I'm giving you an opportunity to recover your job and your reputation. Get back into the good graces of the community and the Westbrooks, so to speak."

I saw red but held my anger in check because losing my cool was never the answer with him. No matter what I did, he always remained unruffled, and I left the conversation looking like an absolute lunatic.

So I just waited. Waited the man out, trying to figure out what the hell his angle was this time around.

He shifted uncomfortably, unused to my forbearance, then he leaned forward. "I have a job offer for you. It's a good position, Harper. You'd be handling campaign PR for the Westbrooks, covering the Congressman's activities."

The words hit me like a physical blow. "You want me to work for the Westbrooks?" I hissed, disbelief coloring my tone.

"It's a good opportunity, Harper."

"That's not an opportunity. It's a death sentence."

"Harper, why do you insist on seeing stories that aren't really there? Your accusations have no basis of proof. Don't you remember what nearly happened last time you tried to accuse someone of something despicable without proof?"

I did, and it had been the beginning of the end for me and my relationship with my father.

"Well, I was half right," I said. "My English teacher *was* having an affair. Didn't know it was with you, but there was certainly a story there."

"There was no story, Harper. Just a broken marriage and a man looking for a little happiness. And you nearly accused her of having an affair with a minor—Miles Westbrook, no less. Something that would have ruined her reputation despite it not being true."

"You ever think back to that day, Dad?" I stared at him for a moment, wondering if I was ever going to be able to connect with him on any level that mattered. Any level that made sense. Was there anything even remotely human to connect to?

"In what way?'

"I found mom passed out drunk in the family room when I got home, and I remember feeling so devastated by it because she had been sober for a year. She had been doing so well, and I blamed myself. My immediate thought was that I had done something to trigger her relapse." I shook my head, feeling the tears form and wishing to hell I could stop them because it made me feel weak. "You were the reason she was drunk. You were the reason she relapsed. And you've never taken any responsibility for that. Yet you constantly accuse me of shifting blame."

"Your mother was a grown adult—"

I slammed my hand on the table. "And so the fuck were you!" I held his gaze, trying to get through to him. "So. Were. You."

He grabbed his drink and took a sip, his hand noticeably shaking. He remained silent for a moment after that and then he finally asked, "And how is she? Your mother?"

With that question, all the fight drained from me. There was no point to this. At the end of the day, he would never change because he couldn't. With a narcissist, this was about as good as it got, and it wasn't even his fault. It was a damn behavioral disease that couldn't be reversed.

So I did something I thought I would never be capable of doing. I grabbed his hand and squeezed it, trying to convey all the love, all the hurt, all the regret, in that one gesture.

And miracle of miracles, he squeezed mine back.

"Please tell Congressman Westbrook that I appreciate the offer, but I can't accept."

And then I stood up and walked away.

As I headed toward the exit, I glanced to my left, thinking I saw Reanne out of the corner of my eye. But when I turned my head, searching for her, all I saw were patrons enjoying their Saturday night. Feeling uneasy, I hurried to the exit and made it out the door, trusting my instincts.

It was time to get the hell out of here.

Mikey still waited in the car with the engine idling. As I slid into the passenger seat, I saw Reanne exit the bar and level her gaze right at us.

"Mikey?"

"I see her."

There are some people in this world who give you an

otherworldly feeling of unease. Reanne Westbrook had cornered the market on spook factor. If I'd believed in vampires, I would have labeled her one and staked her right then and there.

Mikey hit the gas, and we peeled out.

"How did she know where you were?"

"My dad, most likely," I said, belatedly putting my seat belt on. "He wanted me to help with Congressman Westbrook's PR."

"Your dad offered you a job working for the Westbrook's? That's messed up."

"I couldn't agree more."

And it troubled me on a lot of levels because it meant my own father was somehow involved with them. In what way, and for how long...well, it was definitely something I needed to figure out.

"I think we're being followed," Mikey said.

I glanced in the rearview mirror, noticing a black car behind us.

"Think you can lose them?"

Mikey appeared affronted. "It's like you don't know me at all."

# CHAPTER TWELVE

## MILES

"REANNE JUST TEXTED ME. Have you seen her?"

Ed looked up at me and shook his head. "She went out."

"Did she say where?"

"Nope." Ed studied his tie for a second and then looked up at me. "Is something going on between the two of you?"

"Not really." I shrugged, trying to act nonchalant. "Why do you ask?"

"She asked the same thing about you just an hour or so ago. When I told her you went out, she left."

I sighed. *Great. I came back to make an appearance and cover my tracks with Harper, and Reanne might be out there following her right now. Truth be told, I wish I hadn't left her at all.*

Harper would have to take care of herself. Her teenage companion seemed streetwise beyond his years, so hopefully he could help.

"Interesting," I said. "Well, if she comes back, let her know I'll either be in my office or at the bar."

The very thought aggravated me. I'd have to stay at the hotel at least until she returned and make my presence known. Otherwise she'd assume–who knew what she would assume?

I headed for the office first and sat at my desk for a moment.

At Frankie's, we'd found a reference to Quinn. My contact had told me to "find Harper Quinn." Did she mean the same thing? What had the recording meant?

Suddenly, I wished I had it here and I hadn't let Mikey take it for safekeeping, but that would have been the most foolish move on the planet.

I hated that Harper was still in town and in danger, but I loved it at the same time. She was good at her job. If anyone could get to the bottom of all of this, it would be her. But her dad? How was he connected?

If I had the code from my handler, if I had the information he'd been trying to deliver, maybe I could have a look.

I opened my computer and did a quick search of the files I did have access to. First, I searched for Quinn.

Nothing came up, not even related to Harper. Not surprising. They would leave that off the public books for sure.

Then I did a quick Google search for Harper's father. There were articles in damn near every paper in Texas, but I wanted images, so I clicked over to that search instead.

Impressive.

His image was everywhere. In most of the photos, he was behind a microphone on a stage or there were his official headshots with a byline. If the man had a private life, surely someone would have dug it up by now. Someone like his daughter, an ambitious reporter with a nose for the truth.

He could see the family resemblance from the images but clicked back to a regular search. The last few years, he had a lot of big political news stories, but they were pretty tame compared to the ones a few pages back on Google.

Mr. Quinn had been a busy boy when he started out. He seemed to have investigated every politician with a pulse. From New York to the Pacific Northwest to right here in Texas, Harper's father had been a hound dog.

There. About five years ago. "Westbrook Family Biggest Money Launderers on the Gulf Coast." by Montgomery Quinn.

I clicked on the article and saw a photo of my father at a rally. He was on stage, but it was one of those shots reporters like to use when they catch you making a horrible face. Dad looked pissed.

The story went on to state what was pure conjecture, but it all sounded pretty damning.

A whole lot like what the FBI had told me to look for. I couldn't help but wonder if this was where it all had started.

I fast-forwarded again.

About six months after that article appeared, Harper's father was more mainstream. No more in-depth reporting pieces on political figures, but instead background pieces on their platforms and family lives.

In-depth, but not very deep. That's the best way I understood it.

*What did that mean?*

His investigation of my family disappeared, and then it didn't resurface until Harper…

Shit. She was in real danger.

Especially if what I suspected about her father was true.

I moved to shut down my computer but changed my mind. First, I changed my password. This time I used a random string of numbers and letters no one could guess. I took a photo of it with my phone and saved it to a password protected note.

"You're being paranoid," I said out loud, and then shut down the machine.

*Maybe,* I thought. *But maybe not. Everything and everyone is suspect at this point. There's only one person I can trust at the moment.*

*Well, technically two.*

*Harper Quinn and Mikey.*

I headed to the bar, and when I turned the corner to go in, I practically ran into Reanne head on.

"Hey, bro, where have you been?"

"Out," I said sharply.

"Join me for a drink?" she asked.

It didn't seem like I had a choice.

♠

I followed Reanne into the bar and waved at Jordan. I held up three fingers, telling him in our own "bro code" what drink I wanted. A Makers Manhattan, half sweet, half dry. He made them better than anyone on this prison of an island.

Reanne smiled at him and stepped up to the bar. "White wine spritzer for me," she said. "And can you keep the drinks coming to us in that booth over there—" She pointed to the large, half-circle booth in the corner, built for more like six rather than two. "And see that we are not disturbed."

Jordan shot me a questioning glance, but I just nodded. This would not be an easy conversation.

Once we had our drinks, I followed Reanne over. She slid in on one side, while I slid in opposite her, facing her across the large table.

"Where were you this evening?" she started.

"I could ask you the same question," I snapped back.

"You were with her." It was a statement, not a question.

"With who?" I knew better than to play dumb, but I needed to know what she actually knew and what she just assumed.

"You know goddamn well who. Don't act stupid with me, Miles. You're already playing with fire."

"What makes you say that?"

"Why is Harper Quinn here?"

"She was covering some sandcastle competition, or something," I said. "She woke up hung over and with a horrible tattoo, and I am just trying to help her find out what happened that night."

"She doesn't remember getting a tattoo? What unethical artist did that one?"

I stayed silent, not wanting to mention Frankie's name. She waited. I waited longer.

"You don't know either?"

I shrugged as an answer.

"I don't believe you." She finished her drink in a single gulp and set the glass down, raising her hand to be sure Jordan saw her empty glass. I decided to pace myself instead, and took a sip, the whiskey pleasantly warming my lips and throat.

*God, that was a good drink.*

"Why would I not tell you if I knew?" I asked, setting my drink neatly on the coaster, and then spinning it left and right.

"Good question. One I would like to know the answer to. Who's the kid?"

I froze but fought to control my expression. "What kid?"

"The one she's been running around with. You met him."

"He's an Uber driver."

"If that kid is old enough to be an Uber driver, I am signing up for AARP. He barely looks old enough to drive."

"I didn't ask him for I.D."

"Maybe you should have before you took him to dinner at The Steakhouse."

"Are you following me?"

She gave me a lopsided grin and folded her arms. "Maybe I just know people."

"Doubtful."

"Did that drink come out of your tie?"

"Jesus!" I said. "You were following me. Or her. Or whatever. Why? What is your deal?"

"You know she was investigating Dad, right? Actually investigating all of us. The whole family. Including you."

"I know."

"And you got her fired."

That one stung. "I did that to get her off the investigation."

"To protect us, or to protect her?" She leaned forward, searching my face. I met her gaze and lashed out.

"To protect us! Who the hell do you think you're talking to, Reanne?" I downed my drink, slammed the glass on the table, and signaled for another without even looking Jordan's way.

"You know what I think?"

"I'm sure you're about to tell me."

"I think you're sweet on her and that it's making you a little blind. But let me open your eyes a bit."

"Oh, please do. Because I am far from sweet on her. I'm trying to help her figure things out so I can get her the hell out of here. Away from us."

"Un-huh. Okay. Whatever you say. Do you know who sent her here and paid for her hotel?"

I did know, but I stayed silent.

"Her editor. Why do you think he would put her up in one of our hotels?"

"I have no idea."

"Guess who else is in town?"

"Who?"

"Her dad." That sent another chill down my spine, and I shuddered as our drinks arrived. I downed half of mine, and, abandoning the idea of pacing myself, told Jordan to bring me another.

"So? Maybe he came to help her out."

"Nope. To offer her a job."

"A job?"

"Do you want to know who she would be working for?"

"Who?"

"Cameron Westbrook and his campaign."

I stared at her in disbelief. "What? Dad offered her a job?"

"Keep your friends close and your enemies closer," she said. "I can't say that I approve, but I don't think she will accept, do you?"

"Not likely."

"That would be my guess, too. So what are we going to do about her?"

"We?"

"Yeah. You seem to have made it past her porcupine demeanor toward all things Westbrook. How are we going to use that?"

She sat back and stared at me. She had me. Either I agreed to work with her to get Harper out of here and off our backs, or I gave away the fact that I was on Harper's side, and if I did...

She would assume I was working with Harper. She might even assume I was working with someone else, trying to bring our family down. While true, I couldn't let her think that for a minute. I was going to have to act like Harper's enemy. Even to Harper herself. Or we would both be in serious trouble or quite possibly killed.

Finding that code mattered now more than ever. I wondered where Harper and Mikey were. What were they doing while I wasted time here with Reanne?

"I'll have to think about it," I said. "She can't be that hard to get rid of."

"It's easier to get rid of Hep-C, not that I would know from experience. But think what you want. Think about it. We'll meet for breakfast in the morning and see if your plan syncs with mine."

"Um, sure," I said, completely unsure.

"With any luck, we'll have her out of here, and this will all be over by tomorrow night."

"Sounds good," I said, draining my drink. "I'll see you in the morning."

I stood and trotted out of the bar, turned right, and headed for my office. I glanced back to see Reanne not far behind, but she took a left toward the lobby.

Slamming my office door behind me, I leaned against it and let out a heavy sigh. I echoed my contact's words in my mind.

*Find Harper Quinn.*

I texted Harper. "Where are you?"

# CHAPTER THIRTEEN
## HARPER

"WHERE ARE WE?" I asked Mikey after reading Westbrook's text. I tried to be heard above the din of the club, but dammit the entire scene was getting on my nerves.

After doing our best to lose Reanne—and not lose my dinner in the process—Mikey had driven us into a parking lot so crammed with cars, it would take Reanne forever to locate ours. And then we scrambled across the street toward this hole-in-the-wall establishment.

Nothing could have shocked me more than Mikey flashing an I.D. that actually allowed him past the bouncer. I stared at the guy. Hard. I was strangely disappointed in his willingness to look the other way with a minor.

The bouncer glanced at me and shrugged. "Mikey can take care of himself, even if he is seventeen."

"Thanks Vance," Mikey said as he grabbed my arm and hauled me into the club.

This kid. Who *didn't* he know?

"Mikey, where the hell are we?" I shouted as the club's noise grew louder. "We should let Westbrook know."

Mikey tried to shout directions a few times, but gave up,

knowing he would never be heard over the thumping of the music's bass. Instead, he grabbed my phone and texted Westbrook the club's address. After a few idiots attempted to grope me, and another guy spilling his drink all over Mikey's shoes, we finally huddled in an obscure corner.

Clubbing.

Not for the faint of heart.

As time passed without Westbrook showing up or responding to my text, the incessant noise, shouting, laughter, and flashing lights ratcheted my nerves to a lose-my-shit level. If I'd had a foghorn in my hand, I would have held it high above my head and let it rip in an attempt to stop time.

It was at that unfortunate moment someone grabbed me from behind. What followed was pure reflex and nearly broke my knuckles.

"Shit, Harper," Westbrook yelled, rubbing his jaw.

"I'm so sorry," I screamed.

"Why the hell would you…never mind. We need to get outta here." He motioned for us to follow.

The club's pulsing beat receded as we pushed through the throngs towards the exit.

"We can't leave yet," I yelled. "Your sister…"

"What?" he screamed.

"Your sister is—"

"A pain in the ass. I left her back at the hotel."

Good to know, but that didn't actually fix anything. I was on her hit list, and my father was in bed with her, or maybe with all of the Westbrooks somehow. At this point, I felt like a moving target, not to mention easy prey.

As we neared the door, Vance held a small UV light, scanning to make sure those who wanted to return had been stamped with the otherwise invisible ink.

As I followed Westbrook past the bouncer, Mikey pulled on my arm.

"Hold up, guys."

"What's wrong?" I asked.

He didn't answer right away but turned to Vance instead. "Hey, man, can you shine that on the tattoo on her shoulder? Just a quick check," he asked.

"What's in it for me, Mikey?"

"Really, Vance?"

"We don't have time for this." Westbrook hurriedly shoved two twenties into Vance's hand, who then directed the scanner toward my tattoo. Under the blue light, a shocking detail emerged—an intricate design on the spade including a skull and some swirls.

"Whoa, that's new," Mikey exclaimed, his tone a mix of awe and curiosity.

"We're gonna need that UV light," Westbrook said.

Vance smirked. "I'm gonna need more money. This ain't mine. It belongs to the club."

Westbrook muttered something unintelligible and handed him what looked like an obscene amount of cash. I did my best to hold back a smart-ass retort about the rich just buying whatever the hell they wanted.

Vance handed it over with a smirk, pulled another one from under the podium he stood behind, and resumed his scanning.

"Let's get to the car and take a look at this. Your tattoo is much bigger than we thought," Westbrook said, his voice tight.

We made our way to Mikey's car while Westbrook scanned the tattoo as we walked, illuminating more hidden details—three playing cards tucked into each other at the top. There was a Joker, a Jack of clubs, and an ace of spades. Under the bottom of the tattoo that had been visible was a pair of ribbons, and each held a series of four letters.

"Why would someone hide part of a tattoo like this?" Mikey wondered.

"It's a message, or a code. Has to be," I said, my mind racing through the possible implications of such a secret embedded into my skin. "Frankie's design book had this slotted under special projects. She's also appears to be in bed with the FBI, and who knows who else. This insane tattoo has to mean something."

"That's what Conners meant," Westbrook mumbled.

Yeah. Find Harper Quinn. No wonder if this was what was on my shoulder.

As we approached the beat up Honda Civic, another vehicle swung into the parking lot, its headlights cutting through the darkness. My stomach knotted as the car passed under a streetlight, illuminating Reanne.

"How did she find us?" Westbrook growled under his breath. "I left her back at the hotel and took a taxi. There is no way—"

"Tracking device?" Mikey suggested, his voice tinged with excitement.

I wanted to shake him for it. This was not a quest for thrills, and my protective instincts were kicking in hard.

"We need to test that theory." Westbrook quickly scanned the parking lot and then motioned for us to get in the car. "Harper, we need to check you for a tracker. It might be somewhere other than on your phone or clothing."

I nodded, feeling a cold prickle of dread. "Let's get somewhere safe first. Then we check everything."

"We may as well drive back to the hotel. If you're being tracked, then that place is already blown. We'll have to relocate either way, but we need that box we found at Frankie's."

Solid plan as far as plans went, but my thoughts reeled. Absolutely none of this made any sense to me. Not the tattoo, not Reanne's sudden obsessiveness with me, not my father's offer of employment…

As if reading my thoughts, Westbrook asked, "What happened with your dad?"

"He offered me a PR job."

"With *my* dad, right?"

I turned to face him and stared at him in surprise. "Was that *your* doing?"

Westbrook shook his head. "It's a power move by dear old Daddy Westbrook, and Reanne does not approve. Especially since she was fairly certain you would turn it down."

"Which I did," I said. I let out a rueful laugh. "And she witnessed it. I wonder if that was a last-ditch effort to play nice."

"But your dad, Harper. What the hell does it mean?"

I didn't want to think about it, but at this point, I had to. "He's probably been in Congressman Westbrook's pocket for a while now. It would make sense, considering how fast he and my boss buried my story last year. I never could understand why my own dad was there at the news station to be the bearer of bad news after I got slapped with that stupid DUI. To sit there and encourage my 'sabbatical,' as he put it." I stared out the window, allowing myself to process that moment again.

"My dad has always been one for chasing a story, even going so far as to steal mine if he could. We were bitter rivals, and when I got fired, I thought he would take up the investigation even though he kept telling me I was chasing shadows. It's been an entire year, and he hasn't made a single move despite the evidence. With my informant dead and his connections and reach, which are far more impressive than mine, he could have easily taken over the investigation ."

Westbrook's brows narrowed. "So you think his concern about you had nothing to do with your DUI?"

I laughed in disbelief. "My father knows me. He knows I would never drink and drive. Especially not after what my mother put us through...he..." I shook my head, feeling an alarming warmth hit my eyes and a sudden itch to call my mom to make sure she was okay. The Westbrooks were known for collateral damage, and my mother might not be safe.

I wasn't much of a crier, but this shit hurt.

Westbrook reached out and grabbed my hand, giving it a

squeeze. I wasn't one for warm and fuzzy, either, but I gripped his hand like it was my only lifeline.

"I thought it was a convenient way to get me off the story so he could move in, but that didn't happen."

"And now we know why." Westbrook waited a beat and said, "I don't regret what I did to try to keep you safe, whether you believe it or not. Maybe your dad was trying to keep you safe, too."

I said nothing, unwilling to believe it was possible. Either way, my dad's strings were now being pulled by Cameron Westbrook.

"How long?" Miles asked, echoing my own thoughts.

"I don't know," I said, "but I intend to find out."

We drove in harrowing silence, each of us lost in thought. I had a really bad feeling about this. It was the same feeling I'd had when I drove out to Nora's to make sure she was okay.

And found her dead in her living room.

With that happy thought haunting me, I called my mom.

♠

Once I checked in and made sure she was okay, encouraging her to take that vacation and go visit her sister, I could finally focus on the task at hand. Back in the hotel room, I dumped my bag, phone, and jacket onto the table.

"Check them all," I insisted.

Mikey took out his phone, opened an app, and started moving it over everything.

"What are you doing?" Westbrook asked him.

"Checking for a blue tooth tracker. It's the easiest way to keep tabs on someone. Can I see your phone, Harper?"

*Polite. Intelligent. Who was this kid?* But I handed the phone over. What choice did I have, really?

Westbrook grabbed the UV scanner and revealed the entirety of my tattoo. It was extremely intricate. Between the original visible ink and the UV ink revealed around the design, it was clear we were looking at something complex.

"I get that this was meant to remain hidden, but we can't crack this if we're always having to scan Harper's arm," Westbrook said. "Mikey?"

"I'm on it." The kid paused in his investigation and took pictures while Westbrook moved the UV light up and down my shoulder and then held it back as far as possible, revealing as much of the tattoo as he could to capture it all in one photo.

"Aha!" Mikey said as he went back to examining my stuff with his phone. "Found it!"

"Found what?" I asked, rubbing my eyes.

He pulled something out of the wallet in my purse. It was thin, about the size of a credit card.

"What's that?" I asked him.

"This is how Reanne has been tracking you. Maybe someone else, too. Who knows?"

"We have to get that box and get out of here," Westbrook said.

"Why?"

"Because I think the key to the code is either in that box, or back at the tattoo shop. And if Reanne followed you here, maybe she'll send someone else. Someone more dangerous. And if they get their hands on that box before we figure out what this tattoo means…" He stopped.

"What?" I asked. "What is it?"

"They might not need you anymore. That tattoo and what it means might be the only thing keeping you alive."

"Okay, but where do we go?"

"I've got an idea. And an idea of what to do with this tracker," Mikey said.

"Which is?" Westbrook asked him.

But before the kid could enlighten us, there was a knock on the door.

# CHAPTER FOURTEEN
## MILES

SOMEONE KNOCKED, and I jumped. Could it be Reanne? Would this be how we proved she was following Harper?

I had an idea. A terrible idea, a thought that maybe, just maybe, there was some way we could figure this out and get Harper out of here. Out of harm's way.

But a part of me, a large part if I was honest, did not want her to go. I wanted her here with me, where I could protect her. If I sent her away…

It wasn't like my father, or hers for that matter, only had reach in Galveston. They'd proven that.

Where could she go to be safe? Was there anywhere?

Truth be told, there probably wasn't. Galveston might be as safe for her as anywhere, at least until we got this resolved. But who could I trust? Not the FBI, that was for sure. My handler disappearing did not inspire confidence, and it led me to believe there was some kind of leak in their organization.

All we had was an Uber driver, and his contacts, whoever they were. We might have had some of my friends, though I wasn't certain of it. Maybe Harper knew someone.

The knock came again and broke my thoughts. We all just stared at the door.

"Well, who's going to open it?" Mikey asked.

Harper's mouth worked like she wanted to say something, but I could tell this had all been too much. The tattoo, the tracker. She couldn't handle one more thing.

Mikey wasn't stepping forward, even though he might be the logical choice. It made sense for him to be here, more sense than me being here, but despite his bravado, independence, and connections, he was just a kid.

A kid.

So I stood, grabbed the knob, and pulled the door open.

Mikey's aunt stood there and looked me up and down.

"Mr. Westbrook?" she asked. "Where's Mikey?"

"Right here, Auntie," he said, stepping forward.

"What kinda trouble did you bring here, kiddo?"

♠

She led us to the office, Harper oddly silent as she followed. She headed to a back room, and we could see that everything had been rifled through: drawers were pulled open, books and knick-knacks knocked off of shelves. It reminded me of Frankie's place but on a smaller scale.

"Was anything taken?" I asked. I really only cared about one thing—that the safe had not been discovered, opened, and the contents of Frankie's box taken. If that had happened…

"The safe is…safe, Mr. Westbrook," she said. "But I'm sure whoever came in was looking for whatever is in that box."

"How do you know? Maybe they were just burglars."

She snorted, and I heard Mikey laugh as well. "Look around," she said. "Look at this hotel and this neighborhood. What in the world would they think we had worth stealing? I've run this place for dang near twenty years, and no one has ever broken in. Besides, the whole neighborhood knows us. Most of them, even the gangs, would stop someone rather than help them."

"She's right," Mikey mumbled.

"Can we all just stop for a minute?" Harper spoke up, her voice high-pitched, maybe afraid, but firm. "Let's not even pretend this was a burglary. We just discovered that someone…" She turned to look at me, and the heat from her glare could have melted a chocolate bar at fifty feet. "Someone has been following me. There's some kind of secret message on my shoulder in a tattoo I don't remember getting. And it appears the FBI is somehow involved. Someone wants what Frankie had, and somehow it involves me."

"Of course you're—" I tried to say.

"I'm not finished yet. The two of you—" She pointed to both Mikey and myself. "The two of you are a part of the problem. You, Westbrook, are a part of the family that is after me. Whether or not you are directly involved, as long as you are with me, I'm tied to the very people hunting me."

"Now hold on," I said. "I've only been trying to protect you."

"Right." She tossed her hair with a tiny little gesture. It was at that moment, I realized how right she was—well, and how gorgeous too. But I was trying to focus, dammit.

By trying to help her, I had put her on Reanne's radar. Maybe not entirely, but I'd certainly solidified her place there and my sister's suspicions of her.

"And you, Mikey. While I love how you've been trying to help me, you've only brought trouble to your family as well as put yourself in danger. I can't protect you and at the same time protect myself."

"Hey!" the kid sniffed, and I could tell her words stung. "You called me. You asked me to drive you places. I'm the one that spotted your stupid tattoo."

"And you might have gotten yourself killed at Frankie's by not listening to me. By hiding that box here, and because I led Reanne or one of her goons here, just look around."

Mikey's aunt nodded, and I had no idea what else to say.

Mikey looked at his feet, or at least where I assumed his feet were under the baggy pants he wore.

"Well," his aunt asked quietly. "What now?"

"Give me the box," Harper said.

"What?" I tried to protest, but she shot me daggers with her eyes.

Mikey looked up at her but right back down again.

"I'm leaving," she said. "I don't want either of you to follow. I'm going to figure this out on my own, and then I am going to the FBI —the real FBI, in Austin or wherever the hell they are around here. This box— this is evidence of something, and maybe they will have enough to do something. Maybe they can protect me."

"What about me?" Mikey asked. I could see literal tears in the kid's eyes.

Someone he thought cared about him was abandoning him again.

"You've been great, kid," she said, moving to him. I thought for a second she would hug him. "But it is time to bring in the big guns. We just can't do this alone."

She turned to me, and I did the only thing I could think of, as impulsive and silly as it felt.

I reached out and pulled her into a hug. She stiffened and resisted, and then melted into my arms for just a minute. It felt right. It felt—normal. God help me. For a second it felt like the beginning of love.

And then she pushed me away.

"Another place, another time," she said. "Good luck, and I hope things work out for you."

I reached out again, and she slapped my arm away. "Motherfucker," she said, this time with no anger or conviction, and I smiled.

"Now, who wants to deal with this tracker for me?"

Mikey practically jumped forward to grab the slim tracking device from her hand, and she let him take it.

"Thanks, kid," she said.

Harper Quinn picked up the box, turned towards the door, and walked out of our lives.

The door of the office slammed behind her.

"Where will she really go?" I asked the room in general.

"I'm not sure," Mikey said with a grin. "But I know how to find out."

## CHAPTER FIFTEEN
### HARPER

CLUTCHING THE BOX TIGHTLY, I felt the weight of its secrets even though I had no real clue what they were. But someone clearly wanted this damn thing. I knew I couldn't linger at the hotel. Mikey and Miles were in danger of becoming as dead as my previous informant. Even though Westbrook acted like he was immune to his family's criminal empire, there was no doubt in my mind that Reanne would off her own brother if she thought there was some benefit.

Sociopath is as sociopath does.

My pace quickened as I reached the lobby, merging seamlessly with the transient crowd into the brisk night.

A taxi idled at the curb, and I slid into the backseat, my heart pounding with a mix of fear and resolve.

"Airport," I said firmly.

I looked back to see if I was being followed. They needed to destroy that tracker and get the hell out of there fast. Didn't matter that the place had already been ransacked. Whoever wanted this box would be circling back for it and any known associates.

I just hoped that by separating, I was leading the chase to me and away from them.

As buildings and streets blurred past, my mind raced with plans. FBI headquarters in West Virginia was my destination, although I had no idea what would happen once I got there, and something seemed to be wrong within their own house if Frankie was out of commission. Westbrook couldn't even contact his own handler. But someone over there had to know what the hell was going on.

And I had no intention of attempting to lamely contact someone over the phone and risk the very real mess that might be.

I had to get there, walk in, and lay everything out, hoping they could untangle the dangerous threads I'd gotten caught in. I thought about my father and the mess he'd dragged himself into.

Had he known where this would lead once he started taking handouts from criminals? It was absolutely unfathomable to me that he would do something like this.

Was he an absolute asshole?

Of course.

But he was a self-preserving asshole who knew how to cover himself like no one I had ever encountered. Being in Cameron Westbrook's pocket had to have been one of the dumbest moves he had ever made in his entire life. He was a hell of a lot smarter than this.

It just did not add up.

And maybe the code, once cracked, was better served here than at the FBI, but that plan had already failed. They needed to try something else before one of us was killed.

The taxi pulled up to the bustling airport entrance. Belatedly, I considered the fact that I hadn't even grabbed my shit from the Seagate Hotel and then telling myself I was a moron. It was a sunk cost. Were my few tattered shirts really that important?

I reached for the taxi door and opened it, eager to escape into the anonymity of the crowd. As soon as my feet touched the pavement, a chillingly familiar voice froze me in place.

"Harper Quinn," Reanne Westbrook called out, her tone laced with a deadly calm.

I turned, heart sinking, only to find her a few paces away, her expression composed. Beside her was the man from my haunting memories—the same one who had drugged me right before my accident last year.

Reanne slowly approached, revealing a gun under her designer jacket.

"You shouldn't have run, Harper," she continued, her eyes narrowing slightly. "It makes you look guilty."

"Guilty? Guilty of what?" I asked, truly perplexed.

Reanne stepped closer, her associate blocking my retreat. "You're going to come with me. You're going to do as I say. And if you play really nice, I just might forget that little street rat you've been running around with."

I bared my teeth, feeling near feral at the thought of her anywhere near Mikey.

"You touch him, and I will end you."

Reanne's lips slid into a broad grin. "I just love it when my victims get sassy. And Harper, you have always been the sassiest of them all." She moved in until our noses were almost touching. "Do you have any idea how many times I've visualized cutting your pretty little face up?"

"During prep school or after?" I asked.

She threw back her head and laughed. It was damn creepy.

Once she recovered, she considered me with those glittering green eyes of hers. I swear to god, it looked like her pupils were slitted.

Or maybe that was just vengeful thinking.

"You are going to be so much fun…to play with."

Her large minion grabbed my arm, both of them flanking me.

"You're fucking nuts, Reanne," I said as she very carefully held the gun to my ribs.

"Late to the party on that one, aren't you, Harper? I think we all know I'm a little bit off."

*Motherfucker!*

As we slide into the back of her limousine—a limousine? Seriously?—Reanne pulled out another fun little item that made my mouth go dry.

"A taser? I think I prefer the gun."

Reanne chuckled under her breath and let a few sparks fly in front of my face. She was certainly all about the showmanship. A real ten on the intimidation factor.

"You ever think we could have been friends in school?" she asked as she held her little toy in front of me.

"Will I get tasered if I answer incorrectly?"

Her eyes widened in fake surprise. "Why Harper Quinn, it's like you don't know me at all." She played with her hair for a moment as her minion stared at her with zealot-like adoration in the seat across from us. "Of course, I prefer honesty. It's not like I inflict pain just to hear what I want to hear."

"Oh, for fuck's sake, Reanne, you'll hurt me either way, so what the hell? We couldn't have been friends because you feel nothing. And instead of attempting to use that superpower for something good, you decided inflicting pain was a better idea. The only thing that ever kept you in check was your brother."

She looked at me like she harbored some delightful secret.

"Are you so certain my brother hasn't always been just as sick in the head as me?"

I stared at her in horror, wondering if I had completely misread the signs when it came to Westbrook.

"You're messing with me."

Her grin grew wider if that were possible. "My brother has been leading you along this whole time. You really think he would ever take your side against his own family? How do you think I found you?"

And after delivering that low blow, the goddamn bitch tased me.

♠

I woke with a pounding in my skull. It was a precursor to one hell of a migraine. Not something I experienced often.

*Shit. Shit. Shit.*

The last thing I remembered was Reanne's special weapon. I imagined her running down the school halls, tasering people left and right, and found it unreasonably hilarious. I began to giggle. I'd completely lost it here.

I tried to reach out for…anything…at this point, but my arms were stiff, and as the haze lifted, I realized why.

I was tied to a chair.

The rope cut into my wrists, expertly knotted, leaving no room for escape. I blinked against the dim light, my vision sharpening to take in my surroundings. I wasn't in a dark, dingy basement, or some isolated warehouse like I'd imagined. No, I was in a hotel room—a nice one.

Lavish, really.

And so it begins…

The Seagate Hotel was lavish too, and just look how that had turned out. I actually wanted a cement floor and steel bars surrounding me. It wouldn't have been so jarring of a reality considering my circumstances.

The soft, golden lighting illuminated cream-colored walls, a plush bed with expensive linens to my left, and elegant furniture strategically placed around the space. The faint scent of fresh flowers lingered in the air. My eyes darted to the window, but thick, heavy curtains blocked out any clue as to where I was. Even so, I knew this wasn't about comfort. It was about control.

And right now, Reanne had all of it.

The door creaked open, and the very devil herself walked in, her heels clicking against the polished floor. She didn't look at all like someone who had just kidnapped someone. She was composed, her expression neutral, though her eyes gleamed with anticipation.

It was damn unsettling.

I was never gonna get over that sense of emptiness I always felt around her. Like the lights were out and nobody was home—other than evil, of course.

She carried a glass of water, which she set on a table within arm's reach—if I wasn't tied up.

"You're awake." Her voice was soft, almost pleasant. But I wasn't fooled. There was no warmth here, only ice.

"Where am I?" I asked, my throat dry, making my voice raspy.

"In a place where no one will find you," she replied, stepping closer. "A place where we can talk. You have answers, and I need them."

Awesome. A psychopath thought I had answers that I most certainly did not. Torture would soon follow and then escalate. And she would enjoy every minute of it.

Reanne knelt in front of me, her eyes searching my face. My skin crawled at the invasion. "Don't play games, Harper. This can be easy or it can be hard. Your choice."

I clenched my jaw. She had me tied up in a five-star prison, and now she wanted to play good cop?

No thanks.

Reanne sighed and straightened, walking toward the window. "Let's not waste time. I know you met with Conners. I know he gave you something before he…disappeared. What was it?"

Conners. The name sent a chill down my spine. The FBI agent who'd been my only connection to understanding any of this. The one person who could've told me why the hell I was tangled up in this mess. But I didn't have any information from him.

"I doubt you will believe this, but I'm gonna say it anyway since there is literally nothing else to say here. I don't know what you're talking about. I have no fucking clue who Conners is."

"Of course you do. The night you claim not to remember."

"That's not a claim. It's a fact. As far as black-out drunk goes, I was three, maybe five sheets to the wind, especially after your minion drugged me."

Reanne tisked. "Yes, that was unfortunate…that my sweet brother was so accommodating as to let you view the security footage…as well as your little excursion from the hotel." She chuckled. "We thought the sedative would work a bit faster. I was certain you were back to investigate the family further, so I figured, why not finish what I'd started a year ago?"

Talking with Reanne like this made me feel like I was having afternoon tea. Her tone was just so pleasant. It made the entire situation worse.

"So you drugged me, hoping I would pass out in the bar, and you could…"

Her eyes widened in surprise. "I have to spell it out for you? Obviously it was my intent to assist you to your hotel room and give you the same death I gave Nora."

Bile hit the back of my throat. It was one thing to think it. To be pretty damn sure as to who had done it, but to actually hear Reanne confess? Had I not been hog-tied to the chair, I would have already ripped her throat out.

I schooled my emotions, knowing reactions from me were like candy to her. She ate that shit up. Always had, and I did not like the thought of her getting off at my expense.

"Imagine my surprise when you managed to get into an Uber and take off. It was not easy to follow you. Fortunately, I had help."

I eyed her in disbelief. "I'm sorry. You actually managed to follow me?"

"Oh, we'd already tagged you at that point. Not too hard, really. I was just so surprised when I spotted Conners entering the same tattoo establishment that you had. Someone I knew for a fact was FBI."

"Who exactly is this guy, and how in the hell would you know he was FBI?"

She examined her nails and shrugged. "Stop playing games here, Harper. How I knew him isn't important. What *is* important is the fact that you met with him, confirming my suspicions. You had the FBI involved in your little investigation? Oh, no, no, no, sweet Harper. That would never do."

*Knew him?*

She'd used past tense there.

I studied her expression. It gave nothing away, but in my gut, I knew she was behind his disappearance.

"I didn't get anything from Conners," I said, forcing my voice to stay steady. "I don't know the man. Never had contact with him, and even if I had seen him in this tattoo place, I wouldn't know because I don't recall being there. You *do* remember the drug you gave me, right?"

Reanne turned, her expression hardening. "Don't lie to me. I have my own network of informants, and a little birdie told me Conners was supposed to give his contact something important—something that can bring my family down. I would like to know what that is."

"Reanne, I know you're skilled at detecting lies and truths, so I'm gonna say this again. Hand to God, I never saw this Conners dude. He did not give me a damn thing. I do not have the key to bringing down your father's empire, and I do not remember what happened that night. If this FBI agent was there to meet with someone, it wasn't me."

"And yet, who else? An investigative journalist…someone who had already made headway by turning one of our accountants against us…someone who clearly had a vendetta and possibly her own intel she'd been sitting on. If not you, Harper, then who?"

Yeah. I knew that answer, but I wasn't about to give Westbrook up. And any lie I told her would be detected easily.

"I think the better question to ask yourself is how you plan to get away with yet another murder. Conners is dead, isn't he?"

Reanne's eyes widened in surprise. "Why, Harper, we gave him every chance to tell us the truth the moment he left the parlor, but he was just so stubborn. Didn't even crack under my expert torture." She let out a sad sigh. "Such a pity, really."

She walked toward me again, circling like a predator, her stilettos clicking softly on the floor. "Do you think I'm stupid? Do you think I don't know what you're hiding?"

My pulse quickened, but I kept my expression blank. She had no idea about the tattoo. In all honesty, I didn't really know much about my tattoo either. Conners and Frankie had definitely hidden something on my person, but damned if I knew exactly how it related to bringing down the Westbrooks' criminal empire.

"I don't know what the information was," I said, my voice firmer now because that, at least, was completely true. "Conners never handed me anything, and I have nothing that can incriminate your family."

Reanne's smile was slow and cold. "You expect me to believe that? You—who've spent the last year chasing every lead on us, digging into my father's business, exposing us at every turn?"

I clenched my fists, the ropes digging into my skin. She wasn't wrong. I had been after her family, following every lead I could find.

"I'm telling you the truth," I said, meeting her gaze. "Conners didn't tell me anything. And again, I reiterate, even if he had, I wouldn't remember. Courtesy of whatever drug your asshole monkey injected in me."

Reanne's eyes flicked over me, assessing, calculating. She thought I had something, but she couldn't be sure of what.

The unspoken threat hung between us. She wasn't done with me. Not by a long shot.

Reanne leaned in closer, her breath warm against my cheek. "You know, I don't believe you," she whispered. "But that's fine. We have time. I'll get my answers. One way or another." She walked over to a large bag on the nightstand and pulled out Frankie's box. "Now tell me all about this little item. It was something I noticed near that tattoo artist's workstation. She and Conners seemed to be extremely invested in its contents."

"You were the one present and conscious for that show, Reanne. Why don't you tell me?"

Her eyes narrowed. "Do you really think I'd approach two agents at once? I stayed in the shadows just outside, patient, waiting."

So she had known Frankie was an agent. The FBI needed to deal with their leaks. "And where was I?"

Reanne started laughing. "Passed out in a chair. Honestly, Harper, a tattoo while drunk? How tacky."

I stilled my expression, shocked that she hadn't actually picked up on the significance of it. Reanne was smarter than this. Why the hell hadn't she considered there might be a clue there?

*Because she thought actual hardware was being transferred. USB device. Something physical.*

*Not a message hidden in a tattoo.*

Reanna tapped my chin, pulling me out of my thoughts. "Come on, Harper. You about to tell me all about this box?"

I let out a tired sigh. "I'm just as stumped as you are."

As Reanne pulled back, she studied me for a moment longer, then walked to the door. "And yet, you went to Frankie's to locate it yourself. And then you hid it for safekeeping until you could make it to the airport. You still wanna pretend you don't know anything about this box?"

I made a show of thinking really long and hard before I said, "It offers one the luxury of a choice between Go-Fish and Poker?"

Reanne's voice took on a dangerous edge. "I don't give a flying fuck about the deck of cards. I want answers." She turned and headed to the hotel door. "And Harper? I always figure out a way to get my answers."

She gave the door a sharp tug and glanced back at me. "You'll stay here until you're ready to talk. Think about your options. You won't like what happens if you keep stalling."

The door shut behind her with a soft click, leaving me alone in the luxurious prison. My thoughts raced, and I forced myself to focus. I had to get out of here. I had to keep the tattoo's importance a secret no matter what.

Didn't matter that Reanne had everything all wrong. She still planned on killing me either way.

But I was not gonna let her get away with literal murder.

Not again.

# CHAPTER SIXTEEN

MILES

"WHERE DO you think she's headed?" Mikey asked me. His eyes shone, but the tears had stopped, thank god.

I looked over his shoulder at the tiny screen on his phone. A dot moved down Seawall Boulevard at speed, likely the cab she'd gotten into. Where would she go to contact the FBI? She'd said their headquarters, or maybe Austin? Would she drive? Even to Austin, the fastest way would be a flight. .

"How'd you do that, anyway?" I asked him.

"When I had her phone, I enabled share location on her maps account, and then shared it with my number."

"Brilliant."

We watched for a moment longer, and then it hit me where she was headed.

"The airport," we both said at the same time.

*Jinx.* Good. She'd be away and out of danger. As much as we needed what she had with her to figure out this entire mess, maybe there was another way.

"It's no use to follow her now," I said. "We've got to try to figure this out on our own."

"I hate to ask, Mr. Westbrook…"

"Mikey, it's Miles. I think we're long passed the Mr. Westbrook thing."

"Okay, um, sure," he said. He glanced at his aunt, who just smiled at both of us. "I'm really hungry, and I don't think well when I'm hungry."

I laughed. Although I had yet to determine Mikey's actual age, he reminded me of myself as a teen. "Sure, kid. Where do you want to eat? Pick the place. We can go over what we know while we chow down."

He smiled at me then, and I felt somehow sure that "chow down" was not the current expression for feeding our faces furiously. He looked lost in thought for a second and then looked up.

"Can we go to that steak place? That food was—" He stopped himself. "Maybe that's too expensive. We can go somewhere else if you want."

"That will be good. I could use a steak. Miss, would you like to come with us?" I asked his aunt.

"No thanks," she said. "Although it's been a minute since a handsome young man asked me out for a steak dinner. I've got work to do here, including cleaning this mess up and getting ready."

"Ready?"

"In case they come back," she said. She opened a drawer of the desk and pulled out what appeared to be a Dirty Harry style .44 Magnum, a silver revolver with a long, sinister looking barrel.

"Clearly not thieves looking for quick money," she said, freeing the cylinder and spinning it. Even with my limited experience with guns, I could see a bullet in every chamber. "Or they missed this somehow."

"I'm sure you'll be safe if anything happens," I said. "But do be careful."

"Oh, I will," she said, setting the pistol on top of a stack of disturbed papers. "Have fun kid, but be careful yourself." She grabbed the back of Mikey's head and pulled him into her ample bosom, planting a kiss on the top of his head.

"I will, Auntie," his muffled response came.

"And you," she said, pointing at me. "I know you didn't drag him into this. It was that woman of yours. But you keep him safe for me, you hear?" She glanced at the pistol on the desk. "Anything happens to him, you're responsible."

"Yes, ma'am," I said. "Let's go, Mikey."

He pulled away from her, but I could see the look of fear on his face before he hid it.

"Yeah. Let's do it."

♠

A few moments later, we screeched to a halt in front of The Steakhouse. I'd never been here this late, and the place looked different in this light. The modern design showed a certain thoughtfulness for surviving the frequent hurricanes that swept through here while retaining a feeling that the building belonged exactly where it was.

We walked into a nearly empty restaurant, though the bar seemed to be full. The host from earlier had been replaced by a young, bored-looking blond with a septum piercing and a daisy tattooed behind her left ear.

I'd never seen her before tonight.

"Help ya?" she asked.

"We need a table."

"Restaurant closes in about ten minutes, but I can seat you at the bar—" She stopped. "Your kid can't go in there, though."

"Sydney, seat them just outside the bar in my section, please." Luke grinned like a cat that had swallowed a mouse. "Twice in one night. What a pleasure. Where's your pretty friend, Miles?"

"She—left," I said, realizing we'd just been here—I checked my watch—something like four hours before, and that we were prepping for a midnight snack, not a dinner. And despite the harried events of the last few hours, or because of them, I was also hungry again.

And thirsty. The kid was driving. There would be nothing wrong with a drink. Or four. At least with Harper in the wind, it was unlikely I'd have one thrown in my face.

"Oh. Too bad. What did you do?"

"Why do you assume I did something?' I snapped.

"Because you always do something," he said, and I had to admit he was not wrong. When it came to women, I could blow a good thing faster than anyone.

Jordan told me it was because deep down, I never really wanted it to work out. I wanted to be alone.

He might not be wrong either.

But this was not the night for self-discovery. No. I needed to figure out what had happened to Conners, who the hell Frankie was, and what the hell that had to do with Harper.

Sydney sat us down, and Luke appeared with an old-fashioned for me and some kind of non-alcoholic concoction for Mikey that looked like a virgin Shirley Temple. "You need something to eat?" he asked. "We have a limited bar menu, but I can get the chef to rustle something up for you."

"You got a good burger?" Mikey asked.

That sounded really good, actually, and I knew for a fact they had an off-menu burger that was one of the best around. But they were limited and usually gone by this time of night.

"You're in luck," Luke said with a flourish. "I bet I can get two of those, one for each of you. Fries? A baked potato?"

"Fries," Mikey said.

"Sure, we'll share an order of those," I said, as I was not a huge fan of that American food group.

Mikey looked disappointed but nodded.

When Luke swished away, the clicking of his heels echoing through the empty area, I turned to Mikey.

"You a fan of detective novels, kid?"

He grinned. "Yep. That and true crime podcasts and stuff."

"Really?"

"Yeah. I read a lot growing up. We didn't watch much television, and while Auntie has lots of them in the motel, she's not a big fan herself. And once I started working…" His words trailed off, and he looked out the windows, a long way away from where we sat now.

I wondered about him. How he'd managed to grow up here, and why such a clearly smart kid had stayed, when so many young people left Galveston after high school, never looking back. Oh, some would return for jobs, but those who stuck around almost always disappointed their parents, working in hotels, restaurants, and on the beach. Many turned to drugs and crime.

But maybe I had it all wrong. Maybe Mikey hadn't graduated yet and had big plans for his life. That notion just didn't sit right with what I knew of the kid.

"Who did you read?"

"You mean where do I read? Galveston has a library, you know. I like Chandler, Agatha Christie, and of course I love all the Sherlock Holmes stories. Asimov's Black Widower series really grabbed me, and I love the waiter who solves crimes."

"Waiter who solves crimes?" Suddenly, I felt under-read and wondered how this kid knew more about classic fiction literature than I did.

"Yeah, like Luke might someday."

"What? I figured you for more of a movie watcher. You know, like Jack Reacher and some of that stuff."

He scoffed. "Those aren't mysteries. They're thrillers. It's not the same."

"He's right," Luke said, and as he slid a couple of plates onto the table, the smell assaulted my sinuses. My stomach growled in response.

"About you solving crimes, or about the Reacher series?"

"Both. Kinda."

"How late are you working, Luke?" I asked.

"I was off half an hour ago. I stuck around to clean up and then planned to spend some time in the bar. You know." He winked.

"What? Why are you—" I gestured. "Oh, never mind. How would you know how to solve mysteries?"

"I'm three years into my criminal justice degree," he said with a wave of his hand. "Not sure what I'll do with it, though. It's a tough world for—someone like me—to work in."

*Damn,* I thought. *I've been here nearly my whole life. I see these people all the time, and I know almost nothing about them. Am I that self-absorbed?*

"Maybe Luke can help us," Mikey said. I looked over at him and saw his mouth full of burger, grease dripping down his chin. At least his shirt was protected by the fancy cloth napkin he'd tucked into his collar.

I turned to Luke, someone I would have said was my friend until five minutes ago, when I actually learned something real about his personal life. "You want to help us, Luke?"

"With what?" he asked.

"A bit of a mystery," I said.

"Sure," he said. His face lit up, and I could see that he had more than just a passion for impeccable customer service as a waiter. He seemed excited. "Just give me a few moments."

♠

I ate quickly, or what I thought was quickly as we waited. Mikey's burger was gone, and he'd eaten most of the fries by the time I decided to surrender. Two bites of my burger remained, but I didn't think I could take another bite, not even a single french fry.

Then Luke showed up. I could see he'd either refreshed his eyeliner and mascara, or it just looked that perfect after what had to be an eight or nine-hour shift. As he sat, I went through a discussion in my head.

How much should I tell him? Could I trust a waiter, who, until this evening, I assumed planned to just make a career of The Steakhouse?

And the kid. Clearly not even college-age, but smarter than anyone would give an underage and likely illegal Uber driver credit for. What the hell was I doing here?

"So, tell me the story," Luke said, setting a fresh drink in front of both of us, sitting down, and crossing his legs. He'd somehow managed to carry his own drink as well, a blended margarita, if I didn't miss my bet.

I sighed. "First, how much you know about my family?"

"I've heard rumors and I can read," he said, a seriousness in his voice I hadn't heard before.

"Okay. Let me just say that my sister, Reanne—"

"Bitch," he added with a smirk, and I could see the Luke I knew lurking behind his curious smile.

I'd never really seen him until that moment. He'd always been my favorite, personable waiter who was quirky as hell, something I liked. Many others thought the same of him. But he was more. Much more.

Mikey laughed.

"Ha, ha. I'm not going to dispute that," I said. "She's—she's involved in something that isn't legal, and I am sure my dad's involved, too. I can't say how, because…"

"The FBI is involved?" Luke said quietly.

"Um, I can't—"

"I see a lot more in this restaurant than snotty people and lousy tips," he said. "No offense. You aren't one of those. Let's just say that most people don't pay attention to the waiter and will talk about damn near anything."

"They see you as a piece of furniture," Mikey said. "Just like the Uber or taxi driver is just a part of the car."

"Exactly," Luke said. "So the FBI is looking into your family. That's been the rumor, and likely been happening for years. What's new?"

"I—I may have been helping them."

"Was helping them?" Mikey said. "Mr. Westbrook, you can trust Luke. Just skip the part where you don't open up because you're afraid. We need his help. Or at least another set of eyes."

"Okay," I said with a sigh. Again, this kid surprised me. Both of them did.

"So you were helping the FBI, and then what?"

I recanted the story, briefly, about the missed meeting with my handler, the cryptic message I'd gotten the night he'd been killed telling me to find Harper Quinn, and then nothing.

Mikey took over and told him about Frankie, Harper, and the tattoo.

"Let me see the tattoo," he said, holding out his manicured hand to take Mikey's phone. "You say you took a picture of it?"

"Yeah," Mikey said, and handed it over.

I yawned. God, I was tired. But I watched as Luke studied the photo. A gold earring dangled from his left ear, and he brushed it out of the way, resting his fist on this jaw.

"This part right here," he said. "This only appeared under UV light?"

"That's right," Mikey said. I just watched as they both studied the image. Luke pinched his fingers across the screen, zooming in.

"Can I ask you something?" he said.

"Sure," I said.

"Did you find a deck of cards anywhere along the way? From Conners or something?"

"There was one in Frankie's box," Mikey said. "We didn't think it meant anything."

"Well, I recognize this," Luke said. "This is a code—a clever one, and a very difficult one to break. What information was Conners supposed to give you, Miles?"

"There's a safe in the hotel. Inside is a thumb drive, but it's encrypted. I can't get in."

"Does that make sense with what you know?"

"All along, we've known that the accounting in the hotel does not add up, along with some other things," I said. "And we know there has to be a true account somewhere. That thumb drive is probably the answer.."

"Well, it's probably linked to whatever this code means," Luke said.

"Probably?"

"I won't know until I decode it. Excuse me for one second," he said.

I noticed my drink and Luke's were both empty. Mikey sipped on his still, and I could tell from the look on his face that he didn't like it.

Luke returned with fresh drinks for all of us, quicker than he should have been.

"Thanks," I said, taking a huge sip of whiskey, relishing the heat of the drink on my throat.

"Maybe, if I have that deck of cards. I'm pretty sure I can," Luke said, taking a large sip of his own drink. "As long as no one has shuffled them or taken out the Jokers."

"Taken out the Jokers?"

"That's how the code works," he said. He yawned. "I can explain better when I show you. Where's that deck at now?"

Mikey and I shared a look. "Harper has the cards," Mikey said. "And the rest of the box from Frankie's."

"Where did she go?"

"Airport," Mikey and I said together.

"Where was she headed to?"

We both shrugged, and Luke looked us over. "She said to see the FBI. Austin, or maybe Virginia, who knows?

"Well, it sounds like you might want to find her and get that deck sooner rather than later."

"Agreed."

"But for now, I need to get some sleep, and from the looks of you two, you could use some, too."

"We could," I said. "Mikey, where is Harper's phone now?"

He opened an app on his own phone. "I don't know," he said.

"What do you mean?" I asked.

He turned it toward me, showing the last location shown as the airport. "She probably turned on airplane mode on her flight. We may not see where she went until she lands."

"Which could be a while."

Mikey nodded.

"Alright. Let's get some rest and pick this up in the morning. Let's go, kid. I have a place we can stay."

"Good luck," Luke said. "You know where to find me when you need me."

As we left, he walked into the bar, his night just beginning.

Mikey sped out of the parking lot and headed for the Seagate Hotel. I'd be damned if I was going to hide in my own town.

Not tonight.

# CHAPTER SEVENTEEN
## HARPER

REANNE ENTERED THE ROOM AGAIN, this time with a purposeful stride. I heard her heels clicking on the polished floor, heavy with intent. I had no idea how long I'd been sitting there, waiting for my imminent demise, but I was exhausted, thirsty, and that meal at The Steakhouse had worn off a long time ago.

She stood over me, eyes hard and calculating.

"Ah, yes, I'd like a double cheeseburger, extra fries, a very large portion of mozzarella sticks, and if you could throw in a chocolate shake, that'd be swell." I gave her a sweet smile and leaned closer, lowering my voice to a whisper. "Add some extra barbecue sauce and you won't regret it. I'm a generous tipper."

Honestly, I was playing with lava here, but I did *not* want it known on my tombstone that Harper Quinn went down whining.

"I don't like being lied to, Harper."

"You can tell a lie from a truth? Just because I'm telling you something you don't want to hear doesn't mean it's a lie."

"You think you can outsmart me? I know you're not stupid. You're good at what you do—too good, actually."

I kept my mouth shut, bracing myself. My wrists ached from the tight ropes, but the throbbing in my head made that discomfort seem trivial. The real pain hadn't started yet.

She pulled a chair over and sat down, just inches away, looking too calm for what I expected was coming.

"I want to know what Conners told you. I want to know what you're hiding. And I want to know now."

"I told you," I said, my voice hoarse. "I don't know anything. I didn't get anything from Conners. I don't even remember what happened that night."

"You're lying," she hissed, her tone dropping to something dangerous. "And I'm done playing games. You might think I'm bluffing, but believe me, Harper, I'm not."

She reached into the large bag she'd brought in with her earlier and pulled out a slim case. Setting it on the table in front of me, she opened it with meticulous care, her movements deliberate. Inside was a series of syringes, each filled with a pale, amber liquid.

I had no idea what was in those syringes, but I had a pretty good guess they weren't designed for anything pleasant.

"Reanne, you shouldn't have. I had no idea we were getting fillers. If you could inject just a bit between the brows, I'd be forever grateful."

Reanne looked at me with a cruel smile, picking up one of the syringes and tapping it lightly. "I gotta hand it to you. Most of the men I've worked on were already crying at this point. You're nothing if not entertaining." She chuckled and pointed to the syringe in her hand. "This is a little something I've used before. Nothing too drastic—at least not at first. But it has a way of loosening tongues. You see, it causes the most excruciating pain you can imagine without doing any lasting damage. Perfect for someone like you who insists on being difficult."

"Your aim is to slowly poison me to death?"

"Oh, of course not. That would be too easy." She lifted the syringe above eye level and scrutinized its contents. "This little concoction is a mixture of capsaicin and a mild paralytic. Capsaicin burns every nerve ending it touches, and the paralytic makes sure you can't thrash around too much. Don't worry—it won't kill you. But it'll feel like it's burning you from the inside out."

"Do you honestly think torturing me is going to get you anything? I already said I don't remember," I shot back, trying to sound brave. My heart was pounding out of my chest, but I couldn't let her see that. Not yet, shit, not ever. "If I knew something, I'd tell you just to avoid whatever the hell is in that syringe."

"I think you're stronger than that. But let's see how long you can hold out." Reanne approached me with the syringe, and I tried to steel myself for what was about to happen.

She pressed the needle to my arm, her hand steady as a rock because of course it was. A damn shame this woman never became a heart surgeon.

She'd actually have to own one first, but still…

"This is your last chance to tell me what you know. What were you and the FBI planning? What did they want from you?"

I swallowed hard, my throat dry. "Reanne, I swear to you, I don't have what you're looking for. I didn't meet Conners. I don't even know who he is. You're wasting your time."

"Speaking of…you'll have plenty of time to think about that as this starts to kicks in." She pushed the plunger down slowly, injecting the liquid into my bloodstream.

At first, I felt nothing. Just the cold prick of the needle. But within moments, a burning sensation spread from my arm, radiating through my body. The pain hit like a freight train, so intense I nearly blacked out.

My muscles spasmed involuntarily, and I couldn't stop the scream that tore from my throat. Every nerve in my body felt like it was being ripped apart, stretched, and twisted beyond reason. My skin felt too tight, my bones felt like they were splintering.

Reanne leaned in close, her voice low. "This is just the beginning, Harper. The pain will start to recede and then come back in waves. Just when you think it's over, you realize it's only just begun." I vaguely clocked her sitting back, watching me as I prayed for an anvil to magically appear over her head and crush her. "You can stop this at any time. Just tell me what I need to know."

"Son of a bitch," I yelled as a more intense wave of pain arrived with a vengeance. I gasped for air, overwhelmed. I couldn't think, couldn't focus on anything but the fire coursing through my veins. I wanted to scream again, but my body was locked in place, trembling uncontrollably. Every second felt like an eternity.

"I don't know…" I managed to choke out through clenched teeth. "I don't know anything…about Conners."

"Liar!" Reanne's calm facade cracked. She gripped my face with her free hand, forcing me to meet her eyes. "I know you met him! I know he gave you something!"

"I don't have anything!" I screamed, the agony making it hard to form words. "I swear!"

Reanne stepped back, her eyes narrowing as she studied me. She didn't believe me, not for a second. But God, was I grateful to be just as clueless as I claimed. I would have cracked in two seconds if I'd actually known anything.

It was a disheartening realization.

"You really want to play it this way?" she asked, her voice icy. "Fine. I have plenty of time. But you won't like what's coming next."

She grabbed another syringe from the case and held it up to the light. "This one's a little stronger. Let's see how you handle it."

"Wait!" I gasped, the pain still tearing through me. "You don't need to do this. I'm not hiding anything."

Reanne's smile was cold and thin. "We'll see about that."

She moved toward me again, and I braced for more, but deep down, I knew no matter what I said, she wasn't going to stop. She was too far gone.

I could see how much she enjoyed this. Whether I knew something or not no longer mattered. She was in the zone, doing her thing, and I was just another one of her victims now. She wouldn't stop until she got her answers.

Or until I was dead.

"Remember?" she said. "This won't kill you."

Shit. Had I been speaking out loud?

I had to find a way out. But right now, all I could do was try to hang on.

The next wave ended, and Reanne smiled at me. "How are you feeling, dear?" Her voice dripped with sarcasm.

I tried to speak, but all I could do was groan.

"Ah," she said. "I see you need some time to recover. Perhaps to think about what you know and claim not to know."

Her high heels clicked out of the room this time, and I found myself alone. And God help me, I tried to think about what I did know, if anything. Maybe if I could give her something, she'd leave me alone or maybe even give me a glass of water.

But before my brain could go anywhere else, I passed out.

♠

I came to and shook my head. I was still alone. The case with the syringes still sat on the table, open. I wondered if I could somehow get free and get a hold of one. Then I could give this bitch a taste of her own medicine.

But my arms and shoulders were stiffer than ever. The tricks they used in the movies to break free of ropes wasn't in my repertoire.

The door opened, and Reanne walked back in. In one hand, she held a bottle of water. In the other, she held my phone.

My phone.

I hadn't even thought about where it might be, or even what might be on it. In the moment, I tried to think. How much had we shared in our messages? What information would she find if she could open it?

"I shut this off when we picked you up," she said, waving it in my direction.

"Thanks. I was looking for that. If I could just make a quick call, even send a text, that would be great."

"You'd think by now you would have learned your sarcasm is a bad idea. You know, you are fun. I can see why my brother likes you." She looked at the syringes on the table and back at me. "Do we need another lesson in why being a smart-ass is a bad idea?"

"No thanks. I think I've had enough for now, but maybe later."

"Okay, let's start with something simple then. Is someone tracking you with your phone?"

"Not that I know of," I said truthfully. But I thought of Mikey and his badass, tech savvy little self.

"Is that a maybe I see in your eyes?"

I stayed silent, not trusting myself to speak.

"Well, let's see, shall we? The code to unlock it, please."

"Would no as an answer work for you?"

"Harper—" She reached for the syringes, and I caved. I admit it. The last dose had nearly killed me. I couldn't imagine what a stronger dose would do.

"2369," I said.

She powered on the phone and typed in the numbers. I saw the screen open. She poked something in the screen and frowned.

"Who is Jeffrey Micheal Stevens?" she asked.

"I don't—" But I did know, I realized, and she put the pieces together just as I did.

"Nevermind, Harper. He's that fucking Uber driver who's been following you around like a puppy. Sharp one, he is. Jared?" She turned to one of her goons and held the phone out to him.

"Take care of this?" he asked.

But she didn't release it right away. "No, I have a better idea. Leave this powered on. Go down to the wharf. Wait for the little punk. My brother might be with him. If he is, take care of the punk first. Then bring my brother to me."

I looked from her to him as he grinned. "Consider it done."

I'd tried to keep Mikey and Miles out of danger. I'd tried to escape, to end this.

And instead, I only brought them right back in to it.

# CHAPTER
# EIGHTEEN
## MILES

I AWOKE WITH A START, feeling disoriented as I tried to place where the hell I was. I heard a soft snore and then a voice saying, "Hold the mustard."

My bleary eyes zeroed in on Mikey, who was curled up in a recliner. I was flat on my back on a couch that had most definitely seen better days.

I swore when I finally remembered we had stayed at his aunt's little bungalow separate from the hotel as we waited for Harper to flip her phone off airplane mode.

"Mikey," I said, wincing at the pain in my head. "Kid, you gotta check the GPS again."

Mikey sprang into action, grabbing his back pocket for his phone like a live wire just waiting to make contact.

After a few moments and a confused look, he showed the screen to me.

"Nothing," he said. "It must either be off, dead, or in airplane mode."

I shook my head. "Not possible. It's...what time is it?"

"It's almost nine in the morning," Mikey said, looking alarmed.

"We overslept! She should have had her phone on by now. Maybe her plane got delayed? Can we check?"

"I don't think the airlines would tell me, and I hope not. If they'd tell me, they might tell someone else, too."

"Well, she did say she would do this on her own. But, how?"

I stared at Mikey, marveling at the way his brain functioned... really just amazed it functioned at all when I'd originally pegged him as not too bright.

"She wanted to go to the FBI. And she wouldn't want to risk anyone intercepting her, so I bet she decided against Austin or anywhere close...I bet she's heading to headquarters."

"In Virginia or something, right?" he asked.

"I think so," I said. "This isn't the type of stuff you learn in school."

"The only valuable stuff I learned in school happened on the playground." He grinned.

Of this, I had no doubt.

I made a few phone calls, asking about flights headed to West Virginia that night and if a Harper Quinn had boarded. Of course, no one would tell me anything unless I was a cop or could prove Harper was either missing, in danger, or I was related to her somehow. .

I tried pulling the Mr. Westbrook name toss, but it didn't get me anywhere. But after some quick research on flights, only one had been headed for West Virginia the night before. Unless she'd been headed somewhere else instead, but my gut told me that was wrong. Everything inside me said she never took off at all.

My stomach twisted into knots, a feeling I couldn't shake. Harper was in danger.

"Mikey," I said, my voice tense. He had been pacing, his own nerves shot. "She didn't get on a plane."

He froze mid-step and turned to face me, his face paler than I'd ever seen it. "What do you mean she didn't get on a plane? We saw her leave in that cab. Where else would she go?"

I shook my head. "If she headed to Virginia, or pretty much anywhere I can imagine she would go, she would have landed by now. And Harper would turn on her phone and get in touch with someone as soon as those hot legs of hers hit the ground."

Mikey's eyes narrowed, and I offered him a smirk before I realized what I'd said. He pulled out his phone. "Something's not right, man. I didn't trust it from the moment she got in that taxi."

"What are you doing?"

He gave me a sideways glance, fingers moving rapidly across his phone. "Checking on the driver. I've got a contact who runs the transportation network around here."

*This kid! Of course he does.*

"Let me see who picked her up."

I watched as Mikey worked his phone like a seasoned hacker, his fingers a blur. After a few minutes, his phone buzzed. He glanced at the screen and his expression darkened.

"Shit."

"What?"

He held up the phone. "The driver said Harper was met by two people at the airport entrance before she could even get inside. One was a woman, tall, reddish hair in her mid-thirties. The other was a man, older, wearing a dark coat."

My stomach dropped. "That's Reanne. And the man—that sounds like the description of the guy in the security footage from the hotel."

Mikey nodded, his face grim. "I knew it. They caught her. She didn't even make it inside the airport."

My chest tightened. Reanne had Harper. It was the only thing that made sense. What the hell was Reanne planning?

"Listen," Mikey said, cutting through my thoughts. "I've got a few other contacts I can reach out to. We can follow Reanne without her even knowing it."

I wanted to learn this kid's networking method.

"Not a bad idea. If she's got Harper, she'll make a move soon.

We just have to be one step ahead of her." My mind raced through possibilities. "We'll follow her. But we have to be careful. If she gets a whiff of us, Harper's life could be in even more danger."

Mikey grabbed his jacket and motioned for me to follow. "Don't worry. I've got people who are good at this. Real quiet. We'll know her every move without tipping her off."

♠

Ten minutes later, we knew where Reanne had been last. She'd chosen a motel other than the Seagate, but a swanky choice nonetheless. We didn't have a room number yet, but Mikey's contact, Slick was working on it, and he said he would get back to us.

Just as Mikey finished texting, I saw his eyes go wide.

"Oh, shit," he said.

"What?"

"Her phone is back on, and it's moving." Mikey turned the screen toward me.

Her phone was indeed moving. The little dot showing its location had moved from the hotel we'd just tracked Reanne to down to Seawall Boulevard heading toward the fisherman's wharf.

My instincts flared again.

"That's not her. They figured out we're tracking her. It's a trap."

"Are you sure?" Mikey asked, but he seemed to doubt his own findings.

"No. But pretty sure. If it is a trap though…"

"What are you thinking?"

"I wonder what Luke is doing right now. And I wonder if he can help us set a trap of our own. If that goon is out and about with Harper's phone, it means he is trying to trap us. But it also means Reanne might be vulnerable. Overconfident."

Mikey scoffed. "Isn't she always overconfident?"

I laughed. The kid wasn't wrong.

"Yeah, but this might be a unique case. Would some of your network like to help us obtain a little more information?"

"You bet they would. This is the most fun some of them have had since the locker room incident..." He trailed off, and while a part of me wanted to know what he was talking about. And then... there was another part that didn't.

"Okay. I have an idea," I said. "It might get dangerous, but it will definitely be fun."

"Okay," he said, drawing out the word. "Tell me what you need."

"First, do you have Luke's number?"

"Yeah. I got it last night. I wanted to contact him outside of work when we found that deck of cards."

Again, this kid. Thinking ahead.

"Okay, first we call him. If he is game to help, we'll set the plan in motion."

I told him what I had in mind, and his eyes lit up, narrowed, and lit up again as I talked. By the time I'd finished outlining my idea, he was pacing the room, giddy with excitement.

There was no way this wouldn't work. Before Reanne knew what hit her, we'd have Harper back, the deck of cards in hand, and then we could figure this thing out and end it once and for all.

But we had to hurry. Who knew what Reanne was doing to Harper and would continue to do to her.

I handled the call to Luke, and he answered on the first ring.

# CHAPTER NINETEEN
## HARPER

"I DON'T SUPPOSE you'd be willing to tell me what time it is?" I asked the minute her dumb minion left.

"Time deprivation is a nice little addition to this session's torture. I mean, does anyone know what time it really is?"

I had no desire to find out how she knew any torture tactics, let alone this one.

"And just what does your bulbous-nosed friend plan to do once he gets to the wharf?"

Reanne picked lint off her shirt. The she-devil had the nerve to look bored out of her mind. "Maim and murder, I hope. It's all he's good for, anyway."

No joke! I held a bitter grudge against that particular idiot. He'd caused my car accident and my DUI charges. If I ever saw him when not hog-tied to a chair, his ass would be grass.

Of course, it was literally the dumbest thing to even consider at the moment. Not when Reanne stood over me with another vile syringe in hand.

"I'm thinking we'll try this again."

"For fuck's sake, Reanne. No matter how many times you stick me, the answer isn't gonna change." My muscles spasmed again and my tongue swelled in anticipation of the pain.

"Hmmm, interesting theory. I say we test it out."

This time, she shoved the syringe into my thigh. The effects were immediate. My vision seesawed as liquid fire seared a path up my leg. I didn't need a map of my veins to know where it was headed. It felt like my entire nervous system lit up and caught fire in the wake of one massive explosion. The scream I released was inhuman. I honestly didn't recognize my own voice, and all the while Reanne stood over me with a look that—in my few lucid moments—I would have dubbed as a sick, twisted and morbid fascination.

God, this crazy bitch was fucking sick.

I felt my toes curl and my fingers flex of their own volition. And all I could think at that very moment was how badly I wanted to start the week over. Possibly play with all of those snot-nosed kids I'd seen in the sandy cat litter, and enjoy a leisurely stroll along some overpriced beachfront property.

I wasn't picky.

After blurting out a choked "motherfucker," I completely blacked out.

♠

I woke to the burning sensation creeping up my arm as Reanne stood over me, syringe in hand. She was watching my every move with that cold, empty expression I'd learned was just her, the true Reanne. Any other expression she faked was something she'd most likely learned how to achieve in therapy.

Too bad the rest didn't take.

"This is your last chance," she purred, her voice as silky as the expensive drapes lining the windows. "Tell me what you know about Conners and the FBI. It doesn't have to get worse."

I bit my lip, too stubborn to give her the satisfaction of a response. I'd already told her everything—or, more accurately, nothing. I might have been proud of myself if I hadn't been so certain that, had I known anything, I would have sung like a canary.

Reanne leaned in closer, and my breath hitched as I saw the syringe hovering dangerously near my skin. Her lips curled into a twisted smile. Just as she was about to press the plunger down, a knock came at the door. Reanne's head jerked up in irritation.

"What now?" she muttered.

I barely held back a gasp of relief as the knock came again, louder this time. I tried to croak out a help, but I coughed instead.

"Room service!" a voice called from the other side of the door.

"Awe, Reanne," I barely choked out. "You shouldn't have. Such a generous hostess."

Reanne's brow furrowed. "I didn't order any damn room service."

I managed a smile, suddenly picturing bacon. "I'll take the Moons Over My Hammy."

"The what?"

"My guess is you've never eaten at Denny's. Too early for flapjacks?"

I highly doubted my reference to the movie *Groundhog Day* would get the level of appreciation it deserved, but a woman being tortured could wish.

Whoever was outside didn't wait for an invitation. The ding of the electric lock sounded and the door swung open, followed by a massive tray of food—an entire feast, really. Silver domes covered plates, and the smell of gourmet dishes hit my nose, making my empty stomach twist painfully.

Talk about torture.

Reanne should have led with this.

The hotel worker, who looked to be in his mid-twenties and

completely oblivious to Reanne's lethal glare, cheerily pushed the food in. He gave us a raised eyebrow at the sight of me tied to a chair.

"To each his own," he said.

The idea that this kid thought we were having kinky sex was so funny to me, I chose to laugh my ass off instead of doing the smart thing.

Like asking for help.

"I said we didn't order anything," Reanne repeated, her voice sharper this time. "Take it back."

The hotel worker raised his hands in mock surrender, still grinning like a fool. "Sorry, ma'am, it's already been paid for. A gift from your father?" He scratched his head. "Something like that." Then he winked and started to back out of the room. "Enjoy!"

Reanne's eyes narrowed, clearly not in the mood for a meal, but at least she didn't kill the kid. As soon as the door clicked shut, she turned back to me, the syringe still clutched in her hand. Her gaze flicked to the food, and she let out a low chuckle.

"Daddy always has been so good to me."

"Your dad is one sick bastard. He uses you like a trained pit bull, but my guess is he doesn't know half the shit you get up to."

She took a step toward me, and in that split second, I saw movement from beneath the massive tablecloth covering the tray. It happened so fast, I barely had time to register it. Mikey shot out from under the tablecloth, his face full of determination as he lunged at Reanne.

He hit her with the full force of a linebacker out to win the Superbowl. The fact that Reanne managed to land on her feet convinced me, in that very moment, of what I had always suspected.

The woman was a damn vampire.

She lashed out at Mikey with the syringe, the needle glinting in the dim light.

I sat there completely useless as Mikey ducked just in time, but

Reanne came at him again. He moved like a panther, with his stealth and grace on display. It was low-key impressive, watching him grab the taser from her belt before she could react. In one smooth motion, he jammed it into her side and let it rip. The shock hit her hard, and Reanne tumbled to the floor, twitching violently.

It was delicious.

"Holy shit," Mikey breathed, dropping the taser and stumbling back, his face pale.

I stared at the crumpled, shaking mess at my feet and let out a cackle.

"This is…the best day of…my…my life. Reanne Westbrook. Tased by a middle-grade Uber driver."

I whooped with laughter as Mikey took a pocketknife out and hacked at the ropes binding me.

"How many times do I gotta say I'm of age?" Mikey grumbled.

"Where's Westbrook?"

"I'm here," said a voice that warmed me more than I liked.

Westbrook came in with Luke and the room service guy on his heels.

As his eyes locked onto mine, filled with worry, a tiny tingle that had nothing to do with Reanne's concoction, hit the base of my spine. He helped Mikey finish cutting the ropes while Luke looked around the place muttering things like "Swanky," "Dear Lord, only the rich," and "Why do I always date low-income losers?"

"Are you okay?" Westbrook asked, his voice gruff.

"I'm fine," I managed, though my arms felt like dead weight after being tied up and dosed for hours. I shot a glance at Reanne, who was on the floor, twitching occasionally from the taser hit. "Thanks to Mikey."

I stared at the hotel worker, trying to figure out why he was standing there, taking in the scene like it was just another Tuesday.

I couldn't remember what day it was, so that might have been accurate.

"Thanks for the assist, man." I held out a shaky hand and he smiled, taking it with enthusiasm.

"Anything for Mikey. He says the word, and I'm there for him no matter what. He's been a friend for years."

"Of course he has." I turned to Mikey. "Seriously, who the hell *don't* you know?"

"Is this it?" Luke said, moving toward the box.

Westbrook walked over and nodded. He flipped it open, frowning as he scanned the contents. "Where are the cards?"

Before any of us could respond, the door made a dinging sound and burst open again. Reanne's associate, bulbous-nose, stood there, his eyes wide as he took in the scene. Westbrook didn't hesitate. He launched himself at the guy, tackling him to the ground in one smooth motion.

"Where are the cards?" Westbrook growled, pinning the man down with a knee to his chest.

The man coughed, trying to wriggle free. "What? Cards? What are you talking about?"

Westbrook's grip tightened. "The deck of cards that was in the box. Where is it?"

Reanne's minion threw a punch that managed to hit Westbrook in the jaw, but Luke was quick, striding over and kicking out with his heels, nailing the guy between the eyes. As the man went down, Luke stood over him and strategically placed his stiletto against his jugular.

"Let's try this again," Luke said, clapping his hands like it was all some kind of game. "Where are the deck of cards that were in the box you took from my sweet friend Harper?"

"Oh, those cards? Me and the boys...we were playing with them."

"Playing with them?" Luke hissed, applying more pressure. "I think we're done here."

He gave the guy one more nasty kick to the face that rendered him unconscious.

I stared at Luke open-mouthed and then turned to Westbrook. "Your waiter friend is terrifying."

Luke paced back and forth next to the unconscious minion. "The cards have to be in the original order! Without them, I can't break the code from Harper's tattoo. No one can."

"What are you talking about?" I asked.

Westbrook's face hardened, and he shot a glance at me. "We showed Luke pics of your tattoo. He thinks he knows how to crack the code hidden there, and the key to it is the deck of cards we found in Frankie's box. We need them. Now."

"We don't have any clue where they are. If he was playing with them, he wasn't doing it here," I said.

My heart pounded as a dull ringing sensation hit my ears. I needed to sleep for a month after what Reanne had put me through, but we didn't have time. We had to find those damn cards. She might've been out of commission for now, but the game had just taken another turn. And it wasn't in our favor.

And at this point, the last thing we could do was go to the police.

"What's our next move?" Mikey asked.

"I'm sorry, but to have all of this hinge on a deck of cards that can't be messed up in any way? That can't be the only deck. Otherwise, we're screwed," I said. "There has to be a contingency plan here. Another way."

"You're suggesting there might be another deck?" Westbrook asked.

I nodded. "Think about it. Frankie has the drawings for the tattoo labeled under special projects. Conners is part of handing off the information to you. The tattoo was a last-minute thing, but probably something they were planning to use for future missions once they perfected some kind of system. They had to use it on me in a pinch because of Reanne, but that wasn't their first thought. Is there a chance that Conners had a duplicate deck considering his involvement?"

"It's definitely something we need to find out."

Luke gave me an appreciative look. "If you don't marry her, Westbrook, I may need to switch teams. There are always two decks when it comes to this code. We just have to find the second one."

"You can switch teams only if you promise to keep the fake eyelashes," I said.

"Oh, sweetie. You've got yourself a deal."

# CHAPTER TWENTY
## MILES

MY PHONE RANG, and as happy as I was to see Harper alive and kicking, and Reanne laying in pain on the floor, this was not over by a long shot. If we didn't find some evidence to use against her—well, we could be up on assault charges and in a lot of trouble.

Nothing that would stick, but something that might delay everything long enough for her and my father to hide evidence, to move the books, to move money, to get away with all of it again.

And again, and again.

*Now that my involvement has been revealed, where will I end up?*

I sure wouldn't own and manage a hotel. I should have thought through some of my next moves before I jumped into this thing with both feet.

I looked at Harper as I answered the phone and suddenly felt sorry for the things I'd done to save her. If she wasn't going to be an investigative journalist, where did that leave her?

Doing stories on sandcastle competitions and getting drunk tattoos, that's where. I swallowed and turned away.

"Westbrook," I said.

"The goon make it back?" the young voice said.

"Yeah, we got him. What did you find out?"

"Well, there was another guy backing him up. Showed up at the pier right after that slab of meat gave up and took off."

"And?"

"And we picked him just like Mikey asked. We got a phone—locked though—a wallet with no ID, but some cash, and a deck of cards."

"Deck of cards?" I asked, sucking in a breath. Everyone in the room turned to look at me, and I put the call on speaker so they could hear.

"Yeah."

"Are they in a box?" My heart beat faster than it should have, and I only hoped it didn't pound out of my chest. Harper looked ready to explode, and Luke stood taller than usual, if that was possible, laser focused on our conversation.

"A box? You mean like the ones they come in?" he asked.

"Yes," I said.

I heard him rustling around on the end of the line, and then he answered. "Yep. It's been opened, but they are in the box."

"Okay. Meet us…" I trailed off. "Mikey, where can we meet your friends around here?"

"The cafe," Mikey said. "Ten minutes."

"Got it," the voice said. "What should we do with the wallet?"

"Bring it with you," I told him. "But you can keep the cash for your trouble."

I heard him whoop loudly.

"See you soon," he said.

"You think there's a chance that deck is still in the right order?" I asked Luke.

"Not according to goon-boy here. If they were playing with it, even if they shuffled it once without knowing what they were doing, it's probably messed up. Still, worth taking a look."

"How will you know?"

"By where the Jokers are," he told me.

"Jokers are out," the goon said from the floor.

"What?" I said, turning to look at him. He tried to sit up, but his eyes rolled back in his head, and he laid it down on his large bicep. "We took 'em out."

"I don't understand any of this. How does a deck of cards, Jokers, and some code have anything to do with my tattoo and getting us out of this?"

"Your tattoo is a message," Luke said. "Or at least I think it is. Using a code—"

"Never mind," I stopped him. "Harp, we will fill you in later. Just trust us that we have to go, and if this goon is right, we have to find the other deck of cards that belongs to this set."

"One question," Harper asked. "What are we going to do with them?"

She pointed first at the goon and then at Reanne, who appeared to be coming around.

"I've got an idea," Mikey said. Luke looked at him and grinned.

"You got any duct tape around?" the kid asked the hotel employee.

"Sure thing!" he said, and disappeared.

♠

Once Reanne and her goon—Jared as Harper called him—were trussed up and gagged, we left them alone. I told the room service guy to keep an eye on them, and I knew he would do his best, but doing so would be nearly impossible for him with his job.

"I'll check back," was all he could offer with a shrug. I thought about leaving Mikey or Luke behind, but I felt like I needed them both.

For someone who'd been going it alone against my whole family for a long time, to suddenly need a team by my side felt—wrong. I thought of Jordan and college football and what that meant to me at the time.

But I'd been the kicker. A part of the team—a vital part, I would argue. But still separate from the rest. Always a bit of an outsider. Dad and Reanne—that was a team. I had been the kicker in the family too, even before I switched sides.

And why had I switched sides? A sense of justice? Because I felt wronged? Or because I felt like an outsider?

Didn't matter now. I'd gone from inside betrayer to right out in the open betrayer. Whatever came before that was over.

This group of misfits—even Harper—were my team now.

"That's the best we can do," I said out loud. "We can't stick around to watch them."

Harper smiled. "You behave now, Reanne. Don't you go anywhere."

Reanne tried to yell something, but all that came out was a muffled mess. She shook her head and strained her arms. Despite whatever else might be said about our competing hotel, they sure had good maintenance supplies at this one.

"Yeah. Stick around," Mikey said with a grin.

Luke sauntered over to her, his hips swaying as his heels clicked across the polished floor. "It's a shame you don't have better taste," he said. "Or I'd keep these." He picked up her shoes. "But as it is, I don't want you getting any bright ideas about using them to escape."

He tapped the heel of one against his hand. "We'll dispose of these on the way out."

I hadn't even thought about the shoes. I smiled as Luke turned and winked at me.

"Guys," Mikey said. "Stop playing around. Let's go."

We all left, locking the door behind us as much as any hotel room was ever really locked. I listened for a second, sure I would be able to hear Reanne's protests or Jared fighting his gag, but if they were making noise, the sound didn't travel through the door.

We hurried to the elevator and then down to the street, heading for the cafe Mikey recommended.

I had little hope this deck of cards would prove useful, and

Luke's expression told me he felt the same. But we had to check, and maybe this deck would hold a clue to what we should be looking for when we went...where? Where had Conners been staying?

My thoughts were interrupted by Mikey's crew. They were a couple of kids dressed in a similar "moving pile of laundry" style. Complete with what I swear was a dryer sheet on the shoulder of one young man.

One of the kids held out the cards and the wallet. All while his other hand stayed balled up in his pocket, gripping the cash haul, surely.

Before I could say a word, Luke grabbed both items with a flourish and a "Thanks."

"Good job, kid," I said. "We appreciate it."

"Sure thing. Mikey, can I holler at you?" the kid said.

He and his companion took Mikey aside, and all I could hear from that direction was a bunch of whispers. Luke flipped through the deck and then groaned. He held it up for me to see, or rather held it down to my level from his outrageous height.

The cards were fanned out, and two of the Jokers were right next to each other in the middle.

"Is that bad?" I asked, looking at his face. His normal smile had been replaced by a thin line, if you could even call it that. Now I understood why the guys and gals adored him. Even tightened, his full lips would have made a movie star jealous.

He nodded. "This deck was shuffled. We might be able to reorder it, maybe, but there is not really enough of the code in Harper's tattoo to make that a real possibility. Even if it were possible, it would take hours. Or even longer."

"So what do we do?"

"Go to the tattoo shop," Mikey said. "There's an apartment above it where Conners was staying."

"How do you know that?" Harper asked.

Mikey shrugged and tilted his chin back toward his friends.

"Seriously. Are there any secrets in Galveston you can't uncover?"

Mikey shrugged again and shuffled his feet, seeming a little embarrassed. The kid didn't take praise well, and Harper tended to—well, be Harper no matter what other people might think.

"If there is another deck, it could be there. Or it might be at Frankie's station," I said. "Luke, are you good to hang with us for a little bit longer?"

"For a bit. I'm going to have to make an appearance at work just after lunch."

"Do you ever take a day off?" Harper asked.

"Nope. Can't afford it."

Harper looked puzzled, but she left it alone. Whatever issues Harper and I had in our pasts, poverty was not one of them, and the world that Mikey, Luke, and even Frankie lived in, was a foreign one to the both of us.

"Alright. Mikey, you drive," I said, almost joking. "How fast can you get us to Asylum?"

He pretended to look at a watch on his wrist that didn't exist. "Less than ten minutes."

"Great," I said. "Let's go."

Mikey's friends took off on foot, and with Harper in the front passenger seat and Luke and I crammed in the back, we headed out.

As comical as the scene was as we screeched out of the parking lot, a sense of urgency and dread came over me.

Something felt seriously wrong, and time was running out.

# CHAPTER TWENTY-ONE
## HARPER

AFTER THAT GOD-AWFUL showdown at the hotel, I was still shaking from adrenaline and whatever poison was in my system. Mikey's sharp left did not offer much assistance in the way of a sedative.

My wrists were killing me. The surrounding bruising was gonna be fun to explain to my mother.

*Shit, my mother.*

I needed to call her and make sure she actually went to her sister's place.

There were a million things I needed to do, like call the police and report Reanne. Then again, I'd have to explain why *she* was tied up and I wasn't. With my luck, the cops around here were probably all on the Westbrook's payroll.

Cops were crooked.

And that's how I justified my recent crimes.

But let's be honest, where Reanne was concerned, I felt completely in the right. Giddy, really.

Mikey hit the brakes, and my wrist smacked against the dashboard as I braced myself. I let out a pained hiss.

"Sorry," he said, his focus so intent on the road, I almost laughed.

My desire to find that second deck of cards overrode my discomfort. As far as I was concerned, Mikey could bust out a James Bond move, pull a lever, and power up some sort of jet engine just to get us there faster.

We needed that deck of cards—there was no question about it. And now that I knew how Conners had been involved that night per Reanne's rather thorough monologuing—how villainously cliché—my drugged night of debauchery made a hell of a lot more sense. He had the other deck. I had to believe that. And even though I needed to sleep for a solid twelve hours, the reporter in me wouldn't rest until I had all the answers laid out.

And all the evidence I needed to finally expose Cameron Westbrook's illegal activities.

"What if the other deck doesn't exist? Or what if it isn't where Conners stayed?" I asked.

"We'll find it," Westbrook said, his voice steady, reaching across the backseat and placing a comforting hand on my shoulder. "We will."

We pulled up to the tattoo shop while the afternoon shopping picked up steam. Looking inside the wide storefront window as Mikey parked, it appeared the place was rather busy. Three tattoo artists were working and from what I could see, each was with their own client.

"Are we all going in?" I asked.

"I'd like to think we've got a little more finesse than that. Stay put." Westbrook got out of the car and sauntered to the front door.

"Hate to see him go. But my oh my, I do love to watch him walk away," Luke said suggestively.

I looked over my shoulder, realizing I'd forgotten Luke had been in the back seat with Westbrook.

"How you holding up?" I asked.

"Aside from the brutal car sickness, I'm fabulous." He pointed to the tattoo parlor. "I would, however, jump that man in a heartbeat. I suggest you do something about that before that man is taken."

My stomach fluttered at the suggestion, and denial hit the back of my throat, causing me to stutter rather than make my denial sound firm and convincing.

Luke just smiled as I struggled.

"You're a real pain in the ass," I finally managed.

"Flattery will get you a free meal, of course. Now, what do we plan to do about our delicious Mr. Westbrook."

"Miles is not my type."

"Oh, Miles, is it? Funny. You don't really call him by his first name very often, do you?"

I stared at Luke, fearing what else might emerge from those pouty lips of his. I looked at Mikey, who wore one of his shit-eating grins.

Talk about an ambush.

Fortunately, or rather unfortunately, the subject in question came sauntering back like he owned the joint and the surrounding blocks. He got in the back seat and directed Mikey to drive.

"What the hell happened in there?" I asked.

"Talked to the same artist who was there last time and showed him a picture of my handler."

"Any hits?" Mikey asked.

Westbrook nodded. "Not only did the guy recognize him, he confirmed what Mikey's friends found out, but they called him Dave. So Conners was clearly renting from him and using an alias."

"Or maybe the name Conners *was* the alias. Either way, where does that leave us?" Luke asked.

"Well, I asked if we could go have a look around, and he not only told me no, but hell no," Westbrook told us.

"But we have to get in there," I said. "We don't have time to wait."

"Actually, we do. So now we find the best damn hotel and crash until this evening when we break in after the shop closes."

I stared at him in disbelief. "Crash? Are you crazy? Reanne is going to be hunting us soon."

Westbrook shrugged. "Then we better use cash and our *own* aliases."

"Westbrook—"

"Harper, you're exhausted. You may act like you're holding up just fine, but you spent the last several hours with my psychotic sister while she did god knows what to you. Something we've yet to unpack, by the way. We are going to a hotel, we are all taking showers, and we're getting some sleep, goddammit!"

"Oh, honey!" Luke said. "You had me at 'best damn hotel,' and as far as I'm concerned, this alpha male act is a major turn on. Please do continue."

"Jesus." I faced forward, barely managing to avoid bumping my wrists into the dash. "Mikey, there's no arguing with stupid. Just do what stupid, I mean, what Westbrook says, and let's get moving."

Luke let out a loud laugh as Mikey reversed. "You three thrill and delight me. Just thought you should know. I'll call in a favor and get my shift covered at work. I wouldn't miss this for anything."

♠

After a bit of driving, and a hell of a lot of arguing, we finally decided on the Moody Gardens Hotel, Spa, and Convention Center of all places. Not exactly discreet, but I guess Westbrook was serious when he said we were crashing in style.

It seemed Mikey was not the only one with friends in helpful places. With a bit of cash, a few aliases, and a nice back door into the hotel, we found ourselves set up with two rooms...and me wishing I had a change of underwear. Commando may be back in, if I can't find something soon.

"Mikey, I will pay you to go downstairs and buy me new clothes," I said as we all rode the elevator to the second floor.

"Not necessary. That's what room service is for," Westbrook said.

I saw Luke give me a meaningful look and tried desperately to ignore it as the elevator dinged on our floor and we exited like the ragtag crew we'd become.

"Mikey, Luke? You guys stay in this room next to me and Harper."

"I'm sharing a room with you?" I sputtered.

"Safety in numbers," Westbrook said. "Besides, you can't share a room with an underaged kid—"

"Not underage—"

"What would his aunty say?" he teased.

I went to smack him, but my arms were all wonky, and he was already opening our hotel door.

"Son of a bitch," I muttered.

Mikey shot me a wink before he disappeared into the room next door.

That kid was always up to something. God help us all if he got bored tonight.

Luke, on the other hand, gave me a slow whistle, looking smug as hell.

"Sugar, take full advantage," he said in a singsong tone.

I stood awkwardly by the door and then straightened my shoulders and walked in. I was a bad-ass journalist. No reason to feel ill at ease. The click of the door seemed louder than it should have, but the room was nice—a dresser, a television bolted to the wall...and a king-sized bed.

One bed.

Shit!

Add to the nice floral scent and my anxiety had now maxed out.

A wave of exhaustion hit me, and I sank onto the mattress, not caring about anything at this point. When I turned to look at

Westbrook, it was to find him standing there, watching me, his expression unreadable. Yet there was something in the way his eyes softened ever so slightly when our gazes met. For a second, I forgot about everything—the danger, the secrets, the way forces far beyond our control had twisted our lives.

"Guess we'll be sticking together for a while longer," he said, his voice low and quiet.

"Yeah," I replied, my throat suddenly dry. "Safety in numbers and all that."

How lame.

I was now repeating his words back to him.

He nodded and moved toward the window, tugging the curtains shut to block out any wandering eyes. The faint glow of sunlight filtered in around the edges, casting shadows across his face as he stood there, looking out at nothing in particular.

"You can take the bed," he said without turning around. "I'll crash on top of the covers, or I can take the chair if you want more space."

I rolled my eyes, feeling the tension in the room shift slightly. "Westbrook, you don't have to sleep in a chair like some kind of martyr. It's a bed. We're both adults. I think we can handle it."

He finally turned, a hint of a smirk playing at the corners of his mouth. "You sure? I'd hate to make you uncomfortable."

I raised an eyebrow. "If I can handle being kidnapped, tied to a chair, and tortured, I think I can handle sharing a bed with you."

That earned me a quiet chuckle. The tension eased a bit, though not entirely. There was something lingering between us, something unspoken. And it wasn't just the danger looming outside or the secrets we both carried. It was…something more.

He sat on the edge of the bed, hands resting on his knees.

"You ever think about high school?"

All the time, but I wasn't about to admit it. I just offered a shrug, not sure where he was going with this.

"I had the biggest crush on you," he continued.

"What?" I had not expected that.

"Yeah." He turned to face me. "I admired you. I liked how determined you were. How you just seemed to know what you wanted. You were born with this innate sense of self that was so damn intimidating. Like nothing could touch you."

I stared at him in shock, allowing his words to envelop me like a warm, comforting embrace.

"It's why I liked you. My life with Reanne and my parents…it all seemed so contrived until I finally figured out that it was. But in a world full of utter bullshit and fake personas, there was Harper Quinn. What you see is what you get. I can't tell you how much I admired that."

"I always thought you and your sister hated me," I said after a few moments of silence.

"Oh, Reanne absolutely did. You always stole her thunder with that school newspaper, and you were teacher's pet. Reanne wanted to be number one, but instead you were and you managed it effortlessly."

"That's not at all true." I gave a rueful chuckle. "I had nothing together. My mom was a recovering alcoholic and my father was such an ass. I looked like I had my shit together at school because everything at home was falling apart. School had to be the place where I actually had control." I paused for a moment, realizing I had never put any of that together until now. "You were the one thing I could never control when it came to high school."

"What do you mean?" His expression said he thought I was full of shit.

I took a deep breath and let it out slowly. "I was attracted to you," I said. "And I did not like it. I didn't want to be one of your fan girls. Didn't want to jump in line, but you shook me up, regardless."

Westbrook leveled his gaze at me. "I guess we both shook each other up."

"And continue to." I flashed him a tired smile, and he returned it with one of his own.

"I still don't get it," he murmured, almost to himself. "How did we end up here, Harper? How did our lives get so tangled in this mess?"

I shrugged, leaning back against the headboard. "Shitty fathers, I guess."

He looked up at me, his brow furrowed slightly. "Yeah...maybe that's part of it."

I shifted, pulling my knees up to my chest as I met his gaze. "Your father...was he always like that? Controlling everything? Running people's lives from the shadows?"

Westbrook's jaw tightened, and he ran a hand through his hair, clearly trying to decide how much to say. "My father...he was always a powerful man. Always had influence. But somewhere along the way, that power got twisted. He stopped caring about people. About what his decisions did to them. It became all about control. It didn't matter who he hurt as long as he stayed on top."

I watched him carefully, the vulnerability in his voice catching me off guard. I'd seen Westbrook as this closed-off, emotionally distant guy who hid behind his power and status. But now, he was letting me see the cracks in the armor. The pieces of himself he usually kept buried.

For the first time, I finally believed that he had wrecked my career to save my life.

And I didn't like it.

"My dad's not much different," I admitted, the words surprising even me. "Except I always thought he was also in control. He had influence, but now he plays the role of a puppet for your father. I just don't get it. I really don't."

For a long moment, we just sat there in silence. It wasn't uncomfortable. We didn't have to pretend, didn't have to be strong or invincible. Just two people, trying to survive the chaos that had become our lives.

Westbrook hesitated for a second, then moved close enough to gently take my hands in his and turn them over, exposing the bruising around my wrists.

"You hurting?"

"I'm fine."

"What did she do to you?"

I let out a heavy sigh that ended in a choked kind of sob. Suddenly, his arms were around me, and I just wept like I hadn't in a truly long time.

He didn't say anything. He didn't tell me it would be okay. He didn't tell me that the pain would go away. Not the pain from my wrists, but the emotional wounds our families repeatedly inflicted. It wasn't okay, but he was there, and I felt safe.

And in that moment, it meant everything to me.

Once I finally calmed down long enough to catch my breath, he pulled back and brushed the tears from my cheeks.

"I'm not sure how we're gonna get out of this, Harper," he said quietly, his voice almost a whisper. "But I'll make sure you're safe. No matter what it takes."

I looked up at him, my heart pounding a little harder than it should've been. "And who's gonna keep you safe?"

He smiled, a sad one that didn't reach his eyes. "I'm not sure anyone can."

Before I could stop myself, I reached out, placing my hand on his heart. The touch was light, almost tentative, but it was enough. He froze for a moment, then looked down at where my hand rested against his chest.

His gaze flicked up to meet mine, and that emotional distance between us continued to shrink, offering a level of connection I think I'd been searching for since high school. We both felt it, but neither of us was ready to name it.

I think we could have, though. We could have easily named it and acted on it, but maybe we both knew that now was simply not the time, and now would have been for all the wrong reasons.

He stood then and pulled the blankets back, inviting me to get in.

"I'll stay on top of the covers," he said with a wry smile. "Wouldn't want to give Mikey and Luke the wrong impression."

I laughed and rolled my eyes, but my heart was still pounding. "Right. Wouldn't want that."

I quickly maneuvered myself under them, my body finally relaxing as Westbrook stretched out beside me, staying true to his word by keeping a layer of blanket between us. But the proximity… it made me feel safe enough to sleep.

I found a strange sense of peace in it. Maybe it was the warmth of his body so close to mine, or maybe it was just the fact that, for the first time in a long time, I wasn't facing this nightmare alone.

We didn't need to say anything more. There were no grand declarations, no promises of a future. Just the quiet understanding that, somehow, we'd found something in each other—something worth fighting for.

And maybe, just maybe, that was enough for now.

# CHAPTER TWENTY-TWO
## MILES

HARPER FELL ASLEEP. I could not. At least at first. I kept the blanket between us, as promised, but a part of me didn't want to. But now was not the time, not in this high stakes situation. Relationships forged under stress rarely worked out.

Rarely. Not never. But it wasn't worth the risk.

I stopped myself. Wasn't worth the risk? What was I thinking? We'd just revealed that we both had not only looked up to each other but also cared for each other even way back when. Was that why I got her fired to save her?

"Who's going to keep you safe?" she'd asked me.

And I'd told the truth. I didn't know if anyone could. Reanne was tied up, but that wouldn't last. By morning, she'd be free and hell-bent on revenge. My father wouldn't protect me. Likely Harper's father wouldn't protect either one of us, or even be capable of it.

Mikey and Luke? They were our friends now, our team who could help us out of this, but for how long? And if my father and Reanne went to prison, and the Westbrook empire crumbled, what then?

Where would I go? What would I do?

Harper would be recognized for her reporting skills. She had a career she could go back to. True, she would need some protection for a while. My father had powerful friends who depended on his network and activities. But they would move on to a new organization, a new supplier, and the heat would die down.

Then Harper would latch on to another story, and then another, and another.

And I would be a pleasant but forgotten memory.

Just a footnote in Harper's autobiography. A washed up football player, son of a prominent mob boss, betrayer of his family, and pretty much unemployable.

I'd have to change my name. Move abroad. Nothing would be the same.

I wished I could be like Harper. I wished at that moment that I could weep, and someone would hold me. I looked at her sleeping form, cuddled so tightly under the covers, a small smile on her lips as she slept.

I slid down in the bed and closed my eyes. She stirred as I did, and her hand made its way out of the covers, landing on my chest.

I smiled. It would have to be enough for now.

Maybe after this, we could find a way forward together.

But at the moment, I couldn't see how.

♠

In my dream, I ran through a house, one I knew instinctively was mine, but I had never seen it before. The television spewed the morning news, and I heard my last name, Westbrook, spoken by the announcers in that urgent, breaking news voice.

Someone pounded on the door, and I shouted as I ran, "Give me a minute."

I didn't know how, but I knew I was alone, and that something was terribly wrong.

The pounding continued, and I woke with a start. I sat up suddenly in the bed, realizing I wasn't alone. Harper was right next to me, and my sudden movement woke her as well.

"Where—what?" she said, shaking her head. Her hair bounced around her face, and she blew a strand away from her mouth with a sleepy huff.

The knock came again, not nearly as loud as it had been in my dream, but not quiet either.

"Justaminute," I said, my words running together. I looked down to make sure I was dressed—I hadn't taken my clothes off the night before, and it looked like I'd jumped on a wrinkle bomb to save a company of soldiers.

I stumbled to the door, one of my socks dangling halfway off my foot.

"Who is it?" I asked.

"It's me, Luke," a singsong voice said. "You guys need to get up and get moving."

I yanked the door open to find Luke standing there with a young kid I didn't recognize at first. He appeared to be somewhere around seventeen, a peach fuzz beard decorating his pointy chin. He wore a striped polo, jeans that, while a bit saggy, seemed to fit him overall. His hair was covered by a baseball cap, the Rangers maybe, on sideways, and on his feet were a pair of white sneakers that looked new.

I looked him up and down again, and then he smiled.

"Mikey?" I asked. "What happened?"

"Luke happened," he said.

"I have more than one talent," Luke said. "May we come in? Is everyone—decent?" he said with a wink.

"Yes—I mean, hold on." I shut the door a little and looked back at Harper, who appeared disheveled—she had not undressed either—but decent. She sat on the side of the bed and suppressed a big yawn then nodded.

I swung the door wide, and the boys walked in. She blinked when she saw Mikey as well, and I couldn't help but smile.

"Mikey?" she said. "You look—good."

"Just a few changes," Luke said, looking around the room. "Looks like you two had a pretty calm night." He sounded disappointed, and I hated him for it. Not because of his expectations, but because I shared his feelings.

"We got some sleep," Harper said. "We all needed it."

"Uh-huh," Luke said. "It's time to rise and shine. We need to locate that deck of cards and find a way to resolve all this." He gestured around the room, as if that explained everything.

"Okay," I said, tasting my breath and smelling myself for the first time. If my family's criminal connections hadn't turned Harper entirely off me, my breath and body odor would for sure. "We need to get cleaned up—looks like you guys already have."

"How about we go find some breakfast? We'll give you two an hour or so to get up and ready?" Luke winked again, and Mikey chuckled.

"Twenty minutes will be fine. We just need to shower and do the basics," Harper said. "I'll go first."

She disappeared into the bathroom, and Luke and Mikey looked at me. I shrugged.

"You heard the lady. See you soon."

"C'mon, Mikey," Luke said. "I know the perfect spot."

They left, and I stood in the middle of the room. We had nothing really to change into, but I needed to brush my teeth and a shower wouldn't hurt. I took my shirt off and tossed it on the bed, then did the same with my pants, without really thinking about it. I turned on the television, if nothing else than to check the local news for anything we should know about.

I heard the shower water stop and moved toward the door, listening.

The door opened, and Harper stared at me. "Westbrook, what are you doing?" she asked.

I looked down at myself, lurking there in boxer briefs and nothing else, standing probably too close to the bathroom door.

"I—I heard the water shut off, and I was just checking to see if you were done," I said, realizing how stupid that actually sounded.

She looked like she wanted to put her hands on her hips, but they were busy holding her towel in place. Her hair dripped onto her bare shoulders, and her glare bored into me. I made the mistake of looking down, realizing the towel only reached her mid-thighs and that she was barefoot.

"Eyes up here," she said. "Why are you hanging out so close to the door?"

"I—I don't know," I said. "I'm sorry."

"Sure. Well, in the interest of time, if you wanted to jump in the shower, I'll wait here and then brush my teeth while you wash up."

"Um, yeah," I said. I squeezed past her awkwardly and shut the door without latching it. I turned on the water, which was still hot, shed the rest of my clothing, and got in.

The water felt good, and I allowed myself to bask in it for a moment.

Then I heard noises outside the shower curtain, a humming that seemed to go with the tooth brushing—it sounded like the Happy Birthday song.

I smiled, almost said something, and then ignored it instead, washing up as quickly as I could, trying not to think about Harper out there in just a towel, a mere foot or two away.

This was not the time or place to be thinking about any of that.

Which implied that there would, indeed, be a time and place for it.

A small part of me hoped so, but the realistic part told me that was foolish.

I finished and took a quick peek out of the shower curtain, but Harper was nowhere to be found.

I stepped out, grabbed a towel, dried myself the best I could, and wrapped it around my middle. I realized my clothes were in the other room and cleared my throat.

"Harper?" I asked. Can you—?"

Before I finished the sentence, the door opened, and a slender arm slid through it. My clothes were grasped in her hand, and she dropped them before her arm disappeared and the door latched.

"Thanks!" I said and dressed quickly. My hair and skin were still damp, but it would have to do. With all the other thoughts racing through my head, a new sense of urgency had taken residence there.

We needed to get going or none of my fantasies about the future, or Harper's role in mine, would even be possible. I heard the murmur of voices on the other side of the door.

As I exited the bathroom, I saw Mikey and Luke already waiting. Mikey lounged on the end of the bed, while Luke at his full height, plus heels, stood closer to the door.

On what served as a desk in the hotel room was some kind of breakfast burrito that smelled delightful. Harper sat in the chair that went with it, a giant bite in her mouth. She stopped chewing. "What? I wasn't going to wait for you."

I grabbed my burrito and unwrapped it, digging in.

"So, now we head back to the tattoo shop?"

"Place should be empty," Mikey said. "They don't open until eleven, and I had my people check. No one is staying in the apartment."

"Okay," I said. "Let's hope we can find that deck of cards and nobody has messed with it. You ready, Luke?"

"Oh, sweetie. I was born ready."

Harper laughed, and then choked. Eggs and cheese sprayed across her lap.

"Motherfucker!" she said.

She stood, brushed herself off, and we all headed for the door, Mikey twirling his keys around his finger, looking truly like a new man.

Luke followed, Harper after, and I brought up the rear, closing the hotel door behind us.

I felt two things at the same time. A glimmer of hope tempered with the feeling that something was about to go terribly wrong.

# CHAPTER TWENTY-THREE
## HARPER

WE MADE our way back to the hotel parlor as the sun dipped below the horizon. Every moment had my nerve endings ready to fire. To say I was on edge was a massive understatement. Reanne had become the Boogey man. She was out there, circling like a shark, and not knowing where she was—or when she'd strike again—created a certain level of torture that even Reanne might have considered poetic justice.

It really pissed me off.

Westbrook kept a watchful eye on our surroundings as Mikey drove like a well-trained bat out of hell through the back streets of Galveston, taking a convoluted route to avoid any tails. He called it controlled chaos.

I called it utter lunacy.

Luke sat in the front seat, fiddling with his phone, but his mascaraed eyes kept darting to the rear-view mirror. He didn't seem at all nervous, though. I got the feeling he truly enjoyed the intrigue.

When we finally pulled up to the alley behind Frankie's tattoo shop, I realized I'd been picking at my nails until they were down to stubs. The place looked abandoned, and not a single thing about this felt right. I had this awful suspicion that Reanne had placed someone here to look for us, just in case.

It's what I would have done.

I scanned the windows of the building, half-expecting someone to be watching us and sensing Conners' presence, even though that man's body would most likely never be found. Reanne was far too thorough to leave it lying around.

We stealthily moved to the back, and Mikey jimmied the lock on the door with ease. He'd proven useful in more ways than I could count, and I was grateful, even if his shady skills came with some uncomfortable implications.

We slipped inside, and a sense of foreboding hit me hard. Certain smells invited you in. Others encouraged you to take a long walk off a short pier. The musty smell of stale ink and sweat added to my unease.

Westbrook took the lead, guiding us toward the narrow staircase at the back of the shop. The dim lights flickered as we followed him.

"He was staying here, right? Above the shop?"

I nodded, swallowing the lump in my throat. I hadn't known Conners personally, but I felt an odd connection to him—like a thread tied between us by an unseen hand. He had been the last to know the truth, and I was picking up the pieces of his shattered story.

The door at the top of the stairs was slightly ajar, which did not bode well.

"Why is it open?" I asked.

"My guess is Reanne had someone check Conners' things."

"Wouldn't she have already done that?" Mikey asked.

"I'm sure they would have returned if Reanne wasn't able to find whatever it was she was looking for. Obviously, she found nothing since she was most likely looking for a thumb drive. Not a deck of cards," Luke said.

We pushed past the door and stepped inside. The place itself felt as if it was on the verge of giving up. Shadows danced on the walls, casting eerie shapes across the clutter. It was a place where too many secrets had been exchanged.

In truth, it was barely more than a storage closet, converted into a makeshift living space. A bed, shoved into the corner, looked like it hadn't been slept in for days. The sheets were tangled, stained with dirt. Personal items—clothes, papers, bits of memorabilia—were strewn across the floor.

"We need to find that deck," I whispered, moving toward a small nightstand that had seen better days. "Conners would've hidden it somewhere Reanne's people wouldn't think to look."

"Or maybe he left it out in the open, knowing no one would think anything of a simple deck of cards," Westbrook said.

The man made a fair point.

Mikey immediately began rummaging through the debris on the floor, while Westbrook yanked open the closet door, revealing more mess—clothes, boxes, and papers shoved haphazardly inside. Luke was oddly quiet, his gaze sharp as he scanned the room.

We searched in silence, tension building with every passing second. Each overturned drawer and dusty crevice yielded nothing but frustration. The clock was ticking, and I knew we didn't have long.

We took a beat to process.

"Maybe there wasn't a second deck," I said.

"I don't believe it." Westbrook rubbed the back of his head, looking frustrated. "He had a go-box just like Frankie. Wouldn't surprise me if that was where he put the cards."

Then something clicked in my head. "Check under the bed," I said.

"But we already checked there," Luke said.

Mikey, ever the opportunist, dropped to his hands and knees, using his phone's flashlight to peer beneath the mattress. "What am I looking for under here?"

"I remember a story I reported on, an estate sale, when I was first starting out. A real hack job similar to my sandcastle story." I shook my head as Westbrook let out a snort. "Anyway, it was this huge mansion. The guy who'd owned it was some hermit billionaire afraid of his own shadow. He had all sorts of furniture with false bottoms, including beds with compartments underneath."

"You think there's a false bottom underneath the bed?" Westbrook asked. He sounded doubtful.

"Well, you got a better idea?"

"It just seems so cloak and dagger."

I stared at him like he was missing the obvious. "I have a tattoo on my shoulder with a code embedded in it. One that can only be seen with a UV light. Are you fucking serious right now?"

He lifted his hands in surrender and said, "Mikey, scoot underneath the bed and tell us what you see."

He did as he was told, able to clear the space easily. The light from his cell phone flared underneath the mattress. "This is weird. I can't see springs or boards or anything. It's just all thick wood."

"Start knocking on it, kid. Listen for anything hollow sounding," Luke said.

"Hold on," Mikey grunted. He knocked along the bottom of the bed frame, his fist tapping against the wood in a steady rhythm. The sound was dull and solid at first, the usual thud of a thick, old bed. He continued on like that for what seemed an eternity getting to the top far right as my nerves hit their ultimate breaking point.

"Anything?" I asked, my voice edged with frustration.

"There is a fine art to this," Mikey said. "Don't rush me."

Luke let out a chuckle, and I shook my head.

Smart ass.

After a few more knocks, the blessed sound of a hollow thud met my ears.

"Wait, wait. Do that again," I urged, leaning down. Mikey knocked again, his knuckles rapping against the bottom of the frame. Sure enough, the hollow sound came again.

"Got something," he muttered, pressing his hands along the wooden slats.

"Press on the left side of the hollow spot," I instructed, my voice tight with anticipation.

Mikey slid his hand along the left side of the frame, applying pressure to the hollow spot. There was a soft click, barely audible, but unmistakable.

"That's it," I whispered, a surge of adrenaline hitting me. "Now try to slide it."

Mikey pushed. "Holy shit, this is awesome."

"What you got, kid?"

"This panel just shifted open…and…son of a—" Mikey grinned, dragging himself and the box from underneath the bed. "Got it."

"I can't fucking believe that worked," Westbrook said.

My heart pounded as I knelt beside him. The box wasn't just any old thing; it was small, almost like a cash box, but worn with age. There were scratches along the sides, as if someone had previously tried to pry it open.

"Conners' go-box." My voice was barely a whisper.

Mikey set it on the bed and immediately went to work, his fingers moving deftly as if he'd been cracking locks like this for years. It took only seconds before the lid sprang open with a soft click.

Inside, there it was—another deck of cards, pristine and perfectly intact. Along with the deck was a photograph. I reached for it, my fingers trembling slightly as I pulled it out.

My breath hitched. It was a picture of me—or rather, of the tattoo on my shoulder. Taken from an angle that showed every detail of the ink. Conners had known about the tattoo. He'd seen it before he died.

I stared at the photograph, my mind spinning. Conners had taken this, documenting something important—something he hadn't lived long enough to explain.

I passed the photo to Westbrook, who had joined us. He studied it for a long moment, his brow furrowing.

Mikey carefully lifted the deck from the box, flipping through the cards under the faint light. "Looks like they're all here. But now what? How do we figure out what it means?"

Luke stepped forward, his expression grave as he took the cards from Mikey, inspecting them carefully. "We'll know soon enough. But if even one card is out of place…"

The weight of his words hung in the air like a guillotine. If anyone had tampered with the deck, if even one card were missing, we'd be lost. The message Conners had hidden in my tattoo might never be deciphered.

"We need to move fast," Westbrook said, tucking the photograph into his jacket. "Reanne won't be far behind. If she finds us here…"

I didn't need him to finish that thought. We had the cards, and we had the photo. Now it was a race against time to figure out what it all meant before Reanne found us.

Just as we turned to leave, Luke stopped us. "Wait. We need to check the tattoo now. If I can see what I'm working with once more, it will save a little time."

He pulled out the UV light Westbrook had swiped from the bouncer at the club and motioned for me to sit on the edge of the bed.

"This will only take a minute," he said, flicking on the small handheld device.

The familiar buzz of the UV light filled the room, and I felt a shiver run down my spine. Luke hovered the light over my shoulder, illuminating the tattoo.

Westbrook leaned closer, studying the intricate design glowing under the UV rays. The details I couldn't see before were now visible—the ink pulsing with intricate symbols and lines. But there was more.

Luke shifted the light to reveal two ribbons etched faintly onto my skin. Both ribbons had numbers on them—four digits each, forming a sequence.

Just as Luke opened his mouth to say something, the sound of tires screeching outside made us all freeze. Westbrook's hand shot to his gun. "We've got company."

I rushed to the window, jerking back the curtain just enough to see the unmistakable silhouette of Reanne's black SUV pulling up to the shop. Three of her goons jumped out, scanning the area before heading straight for the door.

"Shit! Reanne's here," I hissed.

"We need to get out of here. Now," Westbrook barked.

Mikey was already halfway out the door. "I've got the car ready. Let's move!"

We bolted down the stairs, the UV light and cards hastily shoved into Westbrook's jacket. Luke took up the rear, slamming the door behind us as we burst into the alley. The SUV's headlights flashed in our direction, and I knew we had mere seconds before they caught up to us.

Westbrook threw himself into the driver's seat of Mikey's car, gunning the engine just as Reanne's men spotted us. They shouted, sprinting in our direction, but it was too late. Luke landed in the front, and Mikey and I managed to throw ourselves in the back seat as Westbrook screeched the tires. We shot forward, speeding through the narrow alley.

"They're on our tail," Luke shouted, his eyes darting between the rear view mirror and the road ahead.

I twisted around to see the black SUV gaining on us. My heart pounded in my chest. We couldn't outrun them forever.

"Mikey!" I shouted. "You got any tricks up your sleeve kid?"

Mikey grinned, his eyes gleaming with mischief as he reached under his seat and pulled out a small device. "Oh, I've got a few."

He pressed a button, and suddenly, a shit ton of rocks, broken bottles, cans of house paint, and even nails dropped from the back of the car, scattering across the road. The SUV behind us swerved, a tire popping as it hit some debris, sending it skidding into a lamppost.

"Are you kidding me?" I said, looking at him in amazement. "I meant some cool driving trick you could share with Westbrook. Not a James Bond move. Why in the world would you ever need to soup up your car like that?"

"In case of a car chase, obviously." Mikey shrugged.

I stared at him, certain he'd used that getaway move before. I was also certain I didn't want to know what the hell the kid had been involved in before Westbrook and I came into his life.

"Who would install something like that for a minor?"

Mikey appeared offended. "I have connections, Harper. I know people. I thought you'd realized that by now."

Westbrook let out a snort. "Nice work, kid. But as far as teaching me a few tricks, I'm not the one in this car who needs driving lessons."

"Cheap shot," Mikey muttered.

Another set of headlights appeared in the distance. Reanne wasn't finished just yet. And this time, she wasn't taking any chances.

"We need to lose them," I said, my voice tight with fear. "Now."

Westbrook nodded, his grip on the steering wheel tightening. "Hold on."

We took a sharp turn, the car fishtailing for a moment before righting itself. The chase was far from over, and we were running out of time.

# CHAPTER TWENTY-FOUR
## MILES

CAR CHASES in real life are never like they are on TV until they are. The fact that Mikey had some spike device installed, like some spy car, told me more about the young man than I wanted to know.

There were only a couple of reasons for them, and none were legal.

Once he dumped those, things got interesting. We exited a turn, his car fishtailing on what had to be bald tires, the vehicle righting itself by some miracle. Luke let out a whoop of joy, but I paid no attention.

Galveston was not a huge place. We had to get off the main drag and find somewhere to hide quickly.

A childhood of sneaking weed or initiating make-out sessions had taught me where those places were.

"Left here," Mikey said, pointing.

I wondered how he knew about those places or if his choice of turn was just a coincidence.

I took the turn a little more carefully but still at speed, noting we had increased the distance between ourselves and the pursuing SUV, but only slightly.

"You know where the garage is, the one nearer Moody Gardens?"

"Yeah. The amusement park, not the golf course?"

"Yeah. Let's ditch the car and get another one," Mikey said.

"How do you propose we do that?" Harper asked. "I don't need to add grand theft auto to my resume."

"You mean you don't play?" Luke and Mikey said at the same time.

As they laughed, I took another turn, sending Mikey crashing into Harper's lap. I saw him untangling himself in the mirror and felt a moment of jealousy. He should be driving, and I should be back there with Harper, as innocuous as the moment would be.

"Not the damn game!" she said. "How do you propose we get another car?"

"We don't," Luke said. "That's what they will expect us to do."

I darted the aging car around a concrete barrier marking the edge of the parking lot. I could see the SUV behind us, but just barely. They'd dropped back.

Because without another set of wheels, the amusement park was a dead end. Unless a plan—Mikey's or now Luke's—worked, we were technically trapped.

"So what do we do?" Harper asked, twisting in her seat to look behind her.

"We hide in the park, and then…"

Luke outlined a plan, and I couldn't help but smile. A waiter would be the one to come up with the idea that just might save us.

Most of the parking spaces were occupied, but most cars were just pulling in, not leaving. Our timing was good.

"I don't see a garage," Harper said.

On the right was a row of dumpsters, and I slowed just slightly. As we passed the second one, I braked and pulled the e-brake at the same time, hoping it worked on this piece of junk.

It did, surprisingly well, making me think maybe under its

unassuming skin, this little car was more well-maintained and tuned than it seemed.

I lined us up perfectly with "the garage" as we called it. A car-sized space between the two dumpsters, just large enough for us to squeeze into.

I backed in, killing the engine as we rolled to a quiet stop.

"Everyone out," I said.

"How are we supposed to do that?" Harper asked. The doors were almost pinned up against the concrete.

I rolled all the windows down as she spoke.

"Climb. Let's go, boys and girls."

Luke got out first, his thin frame folding in amazing ways. The rest of us followed, Harper nearly falling and muttering a not entirely mute "motherfucker" as she did.

We stood in front of the car. "What now?" I asked Luke.

"Follow me."

We did so on a snaking route through the parked cars, and we got an occasional glimpse of a black SUV making its rounds up and down each row.

Searching.

Between the front row of vehicles and the park entrance, I held by breath as we half walked, half ran next to a random family, trying not to stand out.

We arrived at the gates, and I reached for my wallet when Luke stopped me. "Not like that. This way."

He pushed through a door on our left I hadn't even noticed, and we found ourselves inside a narrow corridor. Steps led downward into darkness.

"Down there?" Harper said.

"Just for a little bit," Luke answered.

Mikey looked pale, and I was none too comfortable myself.

But Harper expressed all of our thoughts in a single word.

"Motherfucker!"

Luke smiled but quickly led the way. And down we went.

♠

The stairwell, if that's what you could call it, smelled of damp despair. The further down we went, the less light there was.

Our footsteps clanged on the metal grates that made up each step, but the sound didn't echo. Instead, it seemed to stop inches from its origin.

We descended with no light until we reached a concrete pier of sorts. Next to it was a channel filled with running water. The landing, if that's what you would call it, was only about three feet wide, and there was no rail between it and the water.

I shivered and knew if I was cold, Harper must be freezing. Mikey stepped up behind Luke, and I turned to find Harper right behind me. I offered my hand, and she took it.

The chill of her skin on my warm palm sent a tingle up my arm and into my heart. I followed Luke and Mikey, leading Harper with confidence I did not feel. It seemed like we walked forever, but it couldn't have been more than a couple of hundred yards.

Just two football fields.

Then things got lighter, just a little, and a set of windows to our right revealed that there were rooms of sorts here.

Luke paused at the door of one, listened, and then opened it. We followed him inside.

The light hit me first, an assault on my eyes that took me a moment to adjust. Then I saw we were in some kind of a lounge or conference room. There were snacks on a side table in a tan wicker basket, a coffee machine with an empty carafe, and a long table surrounded by what looked like comfortable chairs.

"What is this place?" I asked.

"Conference room or employee room," Luke answered. "I haven't always worked at The Steakhouse."

"I see," Harper said.

"There's no time to explain. First things first. Let me see the deck of cards."

Mikey pulled out the box, and set it on the table. Luke removed the cards and opened the box carefully.

He slid the deck out and looked through it. He smiled and put a third of the deck on the table, a joker facing up.

He slid his fingers over the cards and did the same one more time. There were now three piles.

"Mikey, let me see the picture of the tattoo again. Is there a notebook around here?"

Harper walked to a side table and came back with a yellow legal pad and a number two pencil. Luke took it and opened the photo on Mikey's phone, the one showing the groups of letters revealed by the black light.

There were two groups of four: vqfw dtxn.

Luke swiftly wrote it down.

Then he started at the top of the first pile and worked his way down to the first joker. Then the second. He wrote down a number associated with each card as he went. When he finished he had a list that looked completely random:

18, 5, 49, 29, 1, 28, 45, 15, 48, 32, 23, 8, 35, 14, 16, 34, 30, 43, 6, 37, 2, 39, 22, 7, 50, 17, 25, 12, 3, 46, 4, 52, 10, 21, 26, 47, 31, 33, 11, 44, 9, 40, 24, 27, 19, 36, 38, 20, 51, 41, 13, 42

But he got to work and matched first the v, then the q, then the f and the w to numbers:

48, 43, 32, 49, 30, 46, 50, 40

He mumbled the number 26, and his pen flew across the paper, creating a new list.

22, 17, 6, 23, 4, 20, 24, 14

Then he went back to the deck again, talking under his breath.

We all stayed silent, watching in awe.

Then he wrote something:

DLIT CREY.

And tossed the pencil down.

"Shit!" he swore then folded his arms.

He looked at the deck and then at the paper.

"Either the deck is wrong, has been messed with, or I messed up."

I looked at the paper and at him. "That's what the message says? Eight random letters translates to eight random letters? That makes no sense."

"Tell me about it. Let me try again."

Luke tore the paper off the pad, and started over.

Mikey picked it up and stared at it intently. A moment later, I heard the coffee pot gurgle.

"What?" Harper said. "There's no booze, so coffee can't hurt, right?" A second later, the smell of coffee drifted through the room.

Luke stacked the cards and went through the process again, paying no attention to the rest of us. I'd never seen him so focused, ever.

And I looked over his shoulder. The results looked the same as they had before.

"Damn it!" he said, tossing the pencil. It skipped off the table and hit the wall.

"What if you're not wrong?" Mikey said quietly.

"What do you mean?" Luke asked. "What in the world would dlit crey mean?"

"Maybe it's not letters," Mikey said. "Maybe it's numbers."

"Numbers?"

"Or numbers and symbols." He took the original sheet of paper and leaned over the table. Luke watched as his hands moved.

He seemed to only take a minute: 4 12 9 20 3 18 5 25

Luke stared. "The number for each letter of the alphabet. D is number 4 and so on."

"Like a safe combination or an encryption for a hard drive," Mikey said. "If not all numbers, the 4, 9, 3, and 5 could be symbols, like this:" he added a few symbols below the number.

$, (, #, %

"But that seems unlikely."

Luke turned to me. "So there is an encrypted drive, one that has the real books on it. One you have not been able to get into?" he asked.

"Yes. Conners said he had a way in."

"And this is that way!" he said.

"I sure hope so."

"Then let's go get it."

"Right. But how do we get out of here?"

"We go by boat," he said. "Follow me."

Mikey carefully folded the legal sheet he held and slid it into a pocket. He handed the other one to me, and I did the same.

"Just in case," he said.

We followed Luke again, but as we left the room, I heard voices coming from back the way we'd come.

I couldn't make them out, and they didn't seem angry, but I didn't want to stick around to find out who they might belong to.

We walked along the edge of the pier or walkway, whatever you wanted to call it, Luke taking long strides, the rest of us struggling to keep up.

We reached what seemed to be the end, and I looked around. "I don't see a boat," I said.

"It's right there," Luke said, pointing.

I saw a dark, small shadow on the water. I stepped closer, and Luke shined a light on the object.

It was a tiny inflatable, barely big enough for three, let alone four. A large motor was bolted to the rear.

"That?" I asked. "Seems a bit small."

Then a shout came from behind us, and while I didn't recognize the words for sure, it sounded like one of Reanne's goons.

"Now or never," Luke said, stepping aboard. He held out his hand.

Mikey went first, I followed, and then turned to look at Harper.

She glowed in the dark corridor, she was so pale.

"What's wrong?" I asked.

"I don't like boats," she said. "And this is not even a boat. It's a tube.

"Harper," Luke said. "We gotta go."

I saw her take a deep breath. "Mother H. Fucker!" she hissed and stepped aboard.

We found ourselves pressed against one another in a way that might have been exciting at another time in another place. The engine roared to life, and I looked back as we pulled away.

Flashlight beams crisscrossed the water, but none found us.

It didn't matter. The clock had just started again.

And our time was running out.

# CHAPTER TWENTY-FIVE

## HARPER

AS WE RACED across the water, I felt Westbrook pressed against me, helping me feel safe. The water splashed over me, and while we were close to shore, in my mind, we were not close enough. And there was no way we could be safe. Reanne would know where we were headed or would figure it out soon enough.

I shivered, whether from the cold water or the fact that it felt like danger was closer than ever. I leaned into Westbrook, knowing in another time and place, this moment might have been significant.

Call me romantic, although no one ever did.

He looked back over his shoulder at me and smiled, and then I felt his hand squeeze my thigh.

*He probably feels the same as I do*, I thought. But as Luke turned the boat and we bounced over an enormous wave, slamming into the water, I gripped his arm just to hold myself in place. We'd turned toward a marina, one I recognized vaguely, but I trusted that the natives in this case knew where we were going.

In just seconds, the ride was over, and Mikey jumped from the front of the boat onto a dock, tying us up. Luke followed, and then Miles turned to me.

"Ladies first?" he asked. "Or do you want my help getting out of the boat?"

"You go first," I told him.

He hopped from the boat easily and turned, holding his hand out. I reached up and he gripped past my hand to my forearm. I locked my grip on his. He practically lifted me, and then my feet were on solid ground. Or wood, rather.

I staggered for a second, and he put his arm around me.

"You good?" he asked, looking into my eyes.

"Yeah," I said, shaking his arm off, as badly as I wanted it to stay right where it was. "What's next?"

"We head inside," he said. "Let's try to be as inconspicuous as possible, and get to my office. There is a back way."

"Is there anyone here you can trust?" I asked him.

His face darkened. "I don't know. I want to say Jordan, but he manages some of the books for the bar and restaurant. I don't know what he knows, and I'd like to think he'd be on my side, but I have no idea."

"There's no one else?" I asked.

"No. We need to get the thumb drive, decrypt it if we can, and then get it to the FBI."

It didn't feel like much of a plan to me. I mean, where were we going to go? We'd have to leave Galveston to get the information to the FBI, or at least someone we could trust. That had been my plan, before Reanne grabbed me, but I had no evidence, or not enough.

Would this drive really seal the deal?

"So where are we going to go?" I asked.

"Harper," Miles said. "One step at a time."

"Speaking of steps," Luke interrupted. "Shouldn't we get moving?"

"Yeah," Mikey said, shifting from foot to foot. I hadn't ever seen him this nervous. He looked younger than ever in "normal" clothes, and I kicked myself again for getting any of them involved in this.

"Lead the way," I said.

Westbrook grabbed my hand and stepped ahead of the others. Luke followed with Mikey right behind. I had no idea how we would stay below anyone's radar: Luke at six-foot-four and wearing heels, Mikey looking like a fresh-off-the-boat teenager, and Westbrook and I—well, both easily recognizable.

We walked over the sand and onto a street that seemed vaguely familiar to me. We crossed at a light, and then Miles ducked down an alley I hadn't even noticed until we were nearly on top of it. After crossing another street, we entered the alley again, and then found ourselves at a back door. One of those hotel card readers blinked red.

Westbrook pulled his phone from his pocket and held it near the pad, and it turned green.

"Good. At least I'm not locked out. Yet," he said. "Let's go."

The hallway clearly belonged in the Seagate, but I hadn't seen this one before, at least from this angle. There were offices and rooms on both sides, but they appeared to be for staff or housekeeping, not guest rooms. The lighting was dim, the carpet older than that in the other hallways, although it seemed to be the same pattern.

A smell of bleach and chemicals filled my nostrils, and I sneezed.

A collective "Shhh" came from my companions, and I felt like we were all walking on eggshells, treading lightly as if that would disguise our footsteps from anyone watching.

"Camera," Mikey said simply, and Westbrook turned his head slightly and nodded.

"It will be fine," he said. "Reanne couldn't be here already, and we will be in and out."

But it didn't feel that way. I wished I could share his confidence, but I did *not* feel the same. We were being watched, and more than ever, I felt like we needed to hurry.

Westbrook seemed to feel it too and quickened his pace.

We took a right at the end of the hallway, then another left, and Miles stopped at a door that looked no different than the others.

He used his phone again, and it opened with an almost inaudible click.

We found ourselves in an office, and as soon as we were all inside, Westbrook dropped my hand and moved toward a photo on the wall.

He clicked something on the side of the frame, and it hinged open like a door, revealing a safe.

Luke moved past me and sat at the desk. He opened a laptop, and Mikey squeezed beside him.

It took what seemed like forever for Miles to get the safe open, and he handed them a thumb drive.

"Thanks," Luke said, and plugged it in.

Mikey pulled a piece of paper from his pocket and set it on the desk.

Luke tapped the keys, and I moved to where I could see the screen as well but wouldn't be in the way. Miles stood on the other side of them.

In the password bar were the numbers **412920318525**.

Luke hit enter. The little box shook, like when you got your password wrong in almost any software, but then offered a cryptic message.

Three tries remaining.

Luke looked at Mikey, who nodded.

He typed **412(20318525**

Two tries remaining.

**412(20#18525**

One try remaining.

Luke looked a little frightened, his full lips pressed in a tight, pink line.

Mikey had a furrow in the center of his forehead that shouldn't belong anywhere on someone so young.

I held my breath.

"A capital letter, a number, a symbol, and the blood of your firstborn," Mikey said, sending a chill down my spine.

**D12(20#18525**

The drive opened.

"Mother—" I clamped my hand over my mouth before anyone could do it for me.

"Yippee-Kai-Ayy," Luke said quietly.

In front of us were several files of what I assumed were spreadsheets. Luke opened one and scrolled through a bunch of names and numbers.

"Whoa!" Mikey muttered.

"This…this is the stuff. Westbrook, are you seeing this?" Luke asked.

But he looked pale. His eyes were locked on the main door to the office, not the back one we'd sneaked in.

"That's great," he said. "But wrap it up. It's time to go."

He pointed, and I saw a monitor over the door showing the hallway beyond. On the tiny screen, I easily recognized the figure of a woman with two large men.

"Motherfucker," I hissed. Instead of stepping toward the hidden exit, I stepped forward.

"Yes, yes, motherfucker," Westbrook said, grabbing my arm. "Let's roll."

# CHAPTER TWENTY-SIX

## MILES

I TOOK Harper by the arm, not because she needed my guidance, but because I felt like she might go feral and attack Reanne if I didn't. As much as I wanted to see what she might do to my sister, now was not the time and place.

But what would be the time and place? I hoped we would not find out, although it seemed unlikely. There were only a couple of ways to get from Galveston to the mainland. We could fly, but considering Harper's last incident at the airport, it seemed like Reanne would have that covered.

The causeway was another one, but that, too, would be easy to block.

The ferry to Port Bolivar would be the other.

The time on the boat, a mere 18 minutes, would not normally feel like a big deal. But today that seemed like an eternity as sitting ducks. Not to mention the wait times. None of them seemed like a good option.

First things first.

I closed the safe, pressed the button to lock it again, and swung the picture shut. Luke ejected the thumb drive, stuck it in his pocket, and closed the laptop. He moved to leave it on the desk like it had been.

"No!" I said. "Bring it!"

"Whatever you say, big man," he replied with a grin, unplugged the charger, and picked it up.

"Where to, boss?" Mikey asked.

"I—"

"You don't know where to turn, do you?" Harper asked quietly. Her words were gentle, almost kind.

"I've just got to make a choice," I said.

"For now, we just have to get out of here," Luke said.

On the monitor, Reanne reached for the door.

"Goddamn it." I pushed the rear door to the office open, and we darted into the hallway, closing it behind us. I listened for a second, wondering if Reanne would figure out we'd been there and where we had gone.

I didn't know if she knew about this passage, but I also didn't know how she couldn't.

"Go!" Harper said, and we went. Luke led the way this time, heels clicking yet muted by the carpet, and I followed.

We reached the first street, and Mikey grabbed Luke's arm and directed him to the right. We all followed, and I wondered what the kid had in mind. I noticed that as fast as he was walking, he was also texting, or doing something on his phone.

We turned the next corner and a Honda that looked oddly similar to his pulled up to the curb. A young man hopped out and tossed him the keys. Mikey caught them.

"Nice threads," his friend said.

"Thanks, Brady. I owe you," he replied before turning to us. "Let's go."

Without a better idea, we piled into the car, Mikey and Luke in the front, Harper and I in the back.

The tires squealed as we pulled away from the curb. We went around the corner, and Mikey pulled over.

"Where to?" he asked.

"We only have a few choices," I said, ticking them off my fingers as I had done mentally in the office.

"What is the one choice we could make that Reanne is least likely to expect?"

"If I were her, I would cover all of them. She has enough people to do that, doesn't she?" Harper asked.

She wasn't wrong, and her thoughts mirrored mine again. I turned to face her.

"I am open to suggestions."

"I have another idea," Luke said.

"What's that?" I asked.

He and Mikey exchanged a look. "First, we need some disguises. Second, we split up."

"What do you mean?"

Luke explained and I nodded. I could see Harper out of the corner of my eye, grinning from ear to ear.

♠

I'd never seen Luke's apartment before, and it was not at all what I expected. An open floor plan, the living area was huge with two comfortable looking couches. The living room led seamlessly into a dining area with a square table made with dark wood, likely walnut, or something similar surrounded by four mid-century modern looking leather chairs a similar color to the table.

Equipped with the most modern appliances and granite countertops, it had to rival the one in my father's house, and I wondered if—

"Yeah, I own the place. It looks like an apartment, but it's a condo-type situation. It's a long story."

"Whatever the story," Harper said. "This place is wonderful!"

Luke's expression told me it had come at a cost, and that cost might be higher than we thought, but I kept my mouth shut.

"You first," Luke said. "Into the bedroom. I think I have just the thing for you."

He took me into his closet, and I had to admit that the selection there was extensive, and there were a variety of dress sizes available.

"Do you think this is really necessary?" I asked again.

"Would Reanne ever suspect that you, of all people, would dress like this?" he indicated a denim dress.

"No."

"Then like I said, this is one of the easiest ways out."

I spent about ten minutes with him picking out something I thought I could be at least somewhat comfortable in. We chose leather boots with only a small heel, and he stuffed the toes with a pair of wadded up socks to keep them from slipping off my feet.

Once I was dressed, he found a curly blond wig that hid my hair well. He turned me to face the mirror. He shaved my face quickly and applied makeup. At this point, I didn't even recognize myself.

I walked out of the room, playing it up a bit and swishing my hips, hoping Luke's transformation of Harper would take a little less time.

Both of them just stared at me.

"Westbrook?" Harper said.

"Yeah, it's me."

"Well, as long as you don't talk, no one will know," Mikey said.

"Your turn, Harper." Luke motioned for her to follow.

He took her in the bedroom, and a little while later she came out, dressed as a man, her figure hidden well, baggy jeans drooping, her fashion sense mirroring Mikey's when we first met.

"Perfect," I said, clapping my hands. "Now, what about you two?"

"We're not wearing disguises," Luke said. "We're the red herring. We'll get Reanne and her people to follow us, making them think we're leading them to you while you escape."

"Which way do we go?" Harper asked.

Mikey tossed her the set of keys to the Honda.

"You'll take the causeway. Luke and I will lead Reanne to the ferry."

"How will you get them to chase you?"

"Oh, we have a plan," Mikey said, nodding to me. "Don't leave here until you get a text from us, okay? When you do, get over the causeway as fast as you can, and get this evidence to the FBI."

"How do we know you'll be safe?"

Mikey and Luke traded a look. "We'll be careful. You guys do the same."

Harper stood and hugged Mikey. "Don't do anything stupid kid," she said.

She turned and hugged Luke too. "You guys don't have to do this, you know."

"Yeah, we do," he said. "Miles, next time you're at the Steakhouse, I expect a helluva tip."

With that, Mikey and Luke walked out the door.

I couldn't sit down. I paced the apartment, phone in hand, waiting.

# CHAPTER
# TWENTY-SEVEN
## HARPER

WESTBROOK and I sat with our phones clutched in our hands, each tick of the clock echoing in the silent space around us. Every second felt like an eternity. We knew that Mikey's message could come through at any moment, giving us the signal to go. That would mean he and Luke had successfully diverted Reanne and her goons. It was our only chance to make it out of Galveston with the proof we needed to finally take down the Westbrooks and get to safety.

At least, that's what we thought.

I clenched my phone, acutely aware of the weight in my pocket. I hadn't told Miles about the backup plan—about how, just before they left Luke's place, I'd quietly handed the real drive to Mikey. It wasn't that I didn't trust Westbrook exactly. But after everything, I needed to be certain. His father wasn't just a ruthless man. He was a man who left marks on everyone he encountered, his own son included. Until I knew if Westbrook could really make that hard decision between family loyalty and doing the right thing, I needed to be careful with what we had found.

Ping.

Mikey's text appeared on my screen: *They're on us. Go now. Watch your back.*

I showed it to Miles, who nodded. We exchanged a glance and I grinned at his makeup, despite the seriousness of the situation. But neither of us said much as we left the building and moved to the Honda. He'd barely gotten the key in the ignition before he glanced over at me, his expression conflicted.

It was strange, realizing that we were in this together, against his own family. I wasn't sure what his intentions were. But the silent understanding between us—that was real. I could feel it. Still, there was a gnawing hesitation inside me, and I wasn't ready to drop my guard completely.

As we pulled away from the hotel, the silence stretched, heavy with unsaid things. Finally, just as we neared the edge of town, Westbrook spoke up, his voice barely audible over the hum of the engine.

"Harper," he began, hesitating as if he wasn't sure he wanted to say the words out loud. "Can I ask you something?"

I glanced over at him, curious, and couldn't help but grin. "Sure, sweet lips."

He kept his eyes on the road, but smiled. "You don't look so bad yourself, sir."

I laughed, but stopped as his smile faded.

"I'm serious, Harp." There was a flicker of softness in his gaze.

*Harp? Did we have nicknames now?*

"Back in high school, would you have ever considered going out with me?"

I blinked, caught off guard. Of all the things he could have asked, that wasn't what I'd expected. "Going out?" I repeated, giving a small laugh. "You mean…on a date?"

"Yeah." He smiled faintly, looking almost boyish. "I used to wonder."

I looked out the window, my cheeks heating. "I mean…maybe. Probably, yeah. You'd have to promise to wear that dress, though."

He chuckled, a soft, low sound that managed to cut through the tension in the car. "I thought you'd never give me the time of day. Maybe I should have dressed nicer."

I shrugged, half-smiling. "Maybe I just liked a good mystery. I should have asked you out, since clearly I wear the pants in this relationship."

Ha laughed. A genuine smile touched his lipsticked lips, and I saw how truly stunning a happy version of Miles Westbrook could be.

The weight between us shifted slightly, easing just a little as he reached over, his hand brushing mine. It was a small gesture, but there was something grounding about it, something that made the danger we were heading toward feel momentarily distant.

That moment broke when my phone dinged.

*They ditched us,* the text from Mikey read. *I think they're headed your way.*

"Miles," I said. "I think we're in trouble."

We'd nearly reached the causeway, but we had a long way to go.

His lips tightened into a thin line. He knew what that text meant without me reading it to him.

Just as I finished that thought, I noticed two black SUVs closing in on us fast. I tensed, heart pounding, as Miles's expression shifted from soft to sharp in an instant.

His jaw clenched, and he pressed down on the gas, trying to put distance between us and our followers.

"How?" I asked.

"No clue, but they made us out either way. So now we deal with it."

But the SUVs kept pace, tailing us with surgical precision. He maneuvered around cars, swerving onto the shoulder as we sped down the road. No matter how fast he went, their powerful engines kept them right on our tail.

"They're getting closer," I said, glancing over my shoulder. My mind raced, knowing that we'd only have seconds to react if they tried to box us in. "Miles, what are we going to do?"

His eyes narrowed as he checked his mirrors. "Hold on."

He swerved sharply to the right, trying to get around a slower car in front of us, but the SUVs matched our every move, flanking us on either side. In a split second, they pulled closer, one SUV moving to block us from the front while the other fell in behind, boxing us in completely.

Miles cursed, slamming on the brakes and bringing the car to a screeching halt on the shoulder. The SUVs followed suit, their engines idling menacingly as their doors swung open.

Without thinking, I shoved open my door, heart pounding, and scrambled out. I pulled out the thumb drive I always had on my own key ring and held it high above my head. The wind whipped around me, the salty tang of the ocean air filling my lungs as I backed up toward the edge of the causeway. Miles followed, eyes wide with alarm.

"Harper!" he shouted. "What are you—"

"Stay back!" I yelled, gripping the drive tightly and holding it out over the water's edge. I glanced down, heart racing as I saw the churning waves below.

One of the SUVs opened, and a tall, imposing figure stepped out, backlit by the SUV's headlights. My stomach twisted as I recognized Cameron Westbrook.

He approached with a careful, calculated expression, his arms raised in what he probably thought was a calming gesture. "Harper," he said, his voice smooth and coaxing, "let's not make any rash decisions here."

Beside me, Westbrook tensed, his fists clenched, looking more than a little ridiculous as the wind whipped through the long hair of his wig. I saw the pain and frustration in his eyes as he looked at his father, the man responsible for so much destruction.

I steadied my breath and met Cameron's gaze. "I don't know

what kind of game you're playing, but we're done with it. This ends now."

Cameron's expression didn't waver, but I caught a glimmer of irritation in his eyes. "It doesn't have to be this way, Harper. You can still walk away from this, both of you. Nobody has to get hurt. Just hand over whatever you think you've got there."

"Nobody?" I let out a bitter laugh, keeping my grip firm on the drive. "You've ruined countless lives, including your own son's. And you have the nerve to say nobody has to get hurt?"

His gaze shifted to Miles, softening slightly, as if he actually cared, his eyes traveling up and down the disguise his son wore. "Son, you don't understand. This is bigger than any of us."

Westbrook shook his head, anger blazing in his eyes. "Maybe that's true. But this time, you're not getting away with it."

Cameron sighed, and I saw his mask slip just a bit. "You're being foolish, and you look ridiculous. I'm giving you both one last chance. Hand over the drive, and we'll walk away. No harm done. I really don't want to get your sister involved." He gestured behind us, and I turned, seeing Reanne get out of the SUV at the rear.

God, I hated that bitch.

I looked at Westbrook, my heart hammering.

He met my gaze, his eyes intense and unwavering. Slowly, he nodded, his hand reaching out to take mine. And in that instant, I knew exactly what he chose.

And it was right.

I turned back to Cameron, my grip tightening around the drive. "Sorry, Cameron. But I'm not playing by your rules anymore. You want this? Go get it."

And with that, I threw it as hard as I could toward the sandy stretch of beach below us.

The world seemed to slow as the thumb drive tumbled through the air, the wind catching it, carrying it further from us. Cameron's face twisted in fury, his shout echoing over the water. Miles reached for my arm, his eyes wide with disbelief, but I stepped back, keeping a firm grip on his hand.

"Come on," I whispered urgently. "We have to go. Now."

As we sprinted back to the Honda, Cameron's men scrambled to retrieve the drive, Reanne shouting and pointing, directing them. I could only hope that the bait would work—that they'd believe we were no longer a threat.

But I certainly didn't believe Reanne would let us get away. Regardless of what Cameron said, I had no illusions that he controlled Reanne.

Miles and I jumped back into the car, and he floored it, tearing down the causeway as fast as the Honda would go. My heart raced as I glanced out the window, waiting for the inevitable pursuit to begin.

But it didn't come. At least, not right away.

We sped across the causeway, neither of us daring to speak as the lights in the harbor passed in a blur. After a few tense minutes, Miles let out a shaky breath, his shoulders slumping as the adrenaline wore off.

"That was our only evidence, Harper," he said quietly, his voice raw with frustration. "What are we supposed to do now?"

I took a deep breath, fighting to keep the smile off my face. "We're going to be fine."

He shot me a look of disbelief. "Fine? You just threw away everything. There are no extra copies, and as much as it will mess with my father's business, he can still recoup."

I shook my head, finally allowing myself a small smile. "Not everything. I gave the real drive to Mikey."

The car swerved slightly as he processed what I'd just said. "You...what?"

I turned to face him, feeling a strange sense of relief wash over me. "I gave it to Mikey before we left. Told him to keep it safe and stay quiet. No one else knows."

He stared at me, stunned. "Why? Why would you do that?"

I met his gaze, searching his eyes. "Because I knew they'd come after us, once they discovered Mikey and Luke were leading them away from us, not to us. Reanne and Cameron would never believe we gave him the drive. And if anything went wrong…he was our safest bet."

He was silent for a moment, then shook his head slowly, a wry smile tugging at his lips. "You're something else, Harper."

I grinned, feeling a strange warmth spread through me despite everything. "Had to make sure you were on my side, you know?"

He chuckled, reaching over to take my hand. "You've got me, Harper. And this time, I'm not going anywhere."

The Honda's engine roared as Miles pushed it to its limits, weaving through the few late-night cars dotting the causeway. The dark waters stretched out on either side, shimmering faintly beneath the glow of the bridge lights. Despite our best efforts, a glance in the side mirror confirmed that at least one SUV was behind us, relentless and closing in.

"Any ideas?" Miles asked, his grip tight on the steering wheel, knuckles white.

"Just keep driving," I said, my mind racing. "Once we're over the bridge, take the second exit toward the coastal road. We need to get out of here fast."

In that moment, I knew who was in the SUV. Cameron might be taking the time to check out the drive, make sure he had the actual evidence. But one of our pursuers wouldn't have cared. I'd been right.

It was Reanne. Had to be. Evidence or not, she wasn't letting us just drive away.

Miles stared straight ahead in concentration, eyes sharp and focused, and his foot pressed harder on the gas, the car speeding ahead. The SUV didn't let up, engines revving as they matched our pace.

As we finally neared the end of the causeway, Miles veered onto the exit, our car swerving slightly as it hit the curve. The SUV followed, headlights glaring in the rear view mirror.

"We need to lose them before they close in," I muttered, my pulse racing. "Can you manage a few sharp turns?"

He flashed a grin, a hint of his old cockiness sparking in his eyes. "Buckle up."

He swerved down a side street, the car jolting as he took the turn at speed, tires skidding slightly. The SUV slowed to maneuver the curve, and for a brief second, it lagged behind. We wound through several tight turns, a mix of empty streets and dimly lit neighborhoods blurring past, but the headlights reappeared each time.

Westbrook glanced over at me, breathing heavily. "We're going to have to do better than this if we want to shake them."

I looked around, catching sight of a small alley coming up on the left. "Pull in there and kill the lights."

He hesitated for a split second, then swung the car sharply to the left, steering us into the narrow alley. The instant we were in, he turned off the headlights, plunging us into darkness. We sat, holding our breath as the SUV roared past the alley, their headlights slicing through the night. We waited, motionless, watching the road in tense silence.

After what felt like an eternity, the sounds of the engine faded, swallowed by the night.

Westbrook exhaled slowly, his shoulders dropping slightly. "Think we're in the clear?"

"Maybe for now," I whispered, trying to calm my racing heart. "But we need to keep moving. They'll circle back once they realize we're not ahead of them."

He nodded, easing the car forward, and we slipped out of the alley, turning onto a quieter road. The tension between us settled, but the urgency was still there, pushing us onward. We drove in silence, the lights of the city slowly giving way to the emptier roads leading us toward the rendezvous point.

As we neared the turnoff, I took out my phone and texted Mikey: *Coming.*

Only the two of us knew the exact location of our rendezvous. I'd shared it with him before we left, keeping it between us. If we had any hope of safety, it was in sticking to our plan.

I directed Westbrook to turn onto the deserted beach road, the headlights barely illuminating the sand and scattered palm trees as we moved further away from the city. I kept my gaze trained on the horizon, searching for any sign of Mikey or, worse, another SUV.

Finally, in the distance, I spotted a small, nondescript Honda parked just off the road, half-hidden behind a thicket of trees. Relief washed over me.

"There he is," I murmured, pointing ahead. Miles pulled over beside Mikey's car, cutting the engine. We sat in silence for a moment, both catching our breath.

As we climbed out, Mikey emerged, glancing around before giving us a quick nod. "You made it."

"Barely," Westbrook said, running a hand through his hair, his eyes scanning the road behind us. "They're close. We don't have long."

Mikey handed me a small package, his expression tense. "Got something for you."

I took it, peeling back the wrapper to reveal a burner phone, a map, and a flashlight. "Thanks, Mikey," I said quietly, meeting his gaze. He was the only one I could trust with this.

"So," Westbrook said, glancing between us, "what's the plan?"

I looked over the map, tracing a route that would take us inland, weaving through several small, off-the-beaten-path towns before eventually connecting to a highway that would lead us toward the nearest FBI field office.

"We toss our phones, and follow this," I said, showing him the map. "It's out of the way enough to keep us hidden, but if we're careful, it'll get us there."

His eyes narrowed as he studied the map. "We're going to need supplies, gas, food—everything. Reanne and my father, won't give up easily. Especially if they find out what's really on this drive."

"We'll stop at a few out-of-the-way places," I said. "Nothing with security cameras, nothing traceable. Did you get the cash, Mikey?"

He nodded, his face serious, and handed me another envelope. "Luke's already headed back. Just get that drive to someone who can use it."

I squeezed his arm. "Thank you, Mikey. You have no idea how much this means. What are you going to do?"

He gave me a half-smile, shrugging. "I'm gonna have to leave Galveston. I can't go back now."

"Why don't you come with us?" Westbrook asked. "Just until we deliver this drive."

"I—I don't want to be a burden."

"You're not a burden, Mikey. We couldn't have done any of this without you."

He and Westbrook hugged, and it was so weird. Westbrook's skirt billowed in the wind, Mikey dressed like a normal teenager, and me, over here dressed like a man, wiping tears from my eyes.

Mikey turned, and I hugged him, too.

We all climbed back into the car, and Westbrook started the engine, guiding us back onto the dark, empty road. As we drove, I leaned back, feeling the weight of everything settle in my chest. The adrenaline was fading, replaced by a raw, gnawing exhaustion, but we couldn't stop. Not yet.

Westbrook reached over, his hand finding mine in the darkness, giving it a gentle squeeze. "We'll make it, Harper. We'll make it through all of this."

I looked over at him, then back at Mikey, who was almost asleep in the back seat. We'd come this far. There was no turning back now.

# CHAPTER TWENTY-EIGHT
## MILES

HARPER LOOKED RELAXED, finally. Maybe she could trust me after all. Her head leaned against the headrest, and her eyes were closed.

Mikey, the poor kid, almost fell asleep as soon as the car pulled away from the curb. I was worried about Luke, but it seemed that at least we'd lost our pursuers.

I pulled a quick left and looked at the map—not something Google or Apple would have designed as an optimal route, but it made sense. We'd spend no more than a few miles on each stretch of road and would be making frequent turns.

My eyes burned with the need for sleep. I'd been happy to take the first driving shift before we stopped somewhere for food and rest.

I put my hand on Harper's thigh, more for comfort than anything, and she slid her hand over mine without opening her eyes. I had no idea what the future might hold for us, but I knew I wanted us to end up together, even if it was only for a little while.

And what about poor Mikey? He couldn't go "home" to Galveston, at least not until we resolved this mess. And then what?

Would my father be the end of the line, or would his friends and associates be a threat to us forever?

My mind leaned toward the latter, and I wondered what the FBI might be able to do for us. They couldn't protect Conners or Frankie.

Just as I had the thought, I saw a big, black SUV appear in my mirror. It couldn't be. How would anyone find us with these random turns?

Maybe it wasn't Reanne or my father. I mean, there were black SUVs everywhere, right? Hell, the FBI even used them. The secret service. What made me think—?

But my hopes were dashed when I saw the large vehicle swerve around another car and approach us quickly. There could be no illusions now. We were being followed.

But how?

Then I remembered the tracker they'd planted on Harper. My father, or Reanne, or one of their goons must have managed to get one on the car, and that meant it didn't matter how clever the route. Without finding the tracker, we wouldn't get away. At least not forever.

And by now, they must know the drive Harper tossed wasn't the real one, and it didn't take a rocket scientist to figure out where they would head next.

*Now what?*

If I couldn't lose them, maybe I could get them in trouble, or get someone else to intercept them.

I pushed the accelerator all the way to the floor. "What's happening?" Harper asked, sitting up.

"They found us," I replied, and then gripped the wheel tightly.

If there was a cop around, surely we'd be pulled over or chased, maybe even given an escort if we could tell our story.

The SUV closed in, the little Honda we drove no match for the power of our pursuers, even though we would be more nimble in turns for sure.

A side road appeared up ahead, and though I had no idea where it might lead, I made a hard right without slowing or signaling. The SUV raced by the turn, but I saw brake lights. Good.

It would take them time to get turned around. The two-lane road seemed to go straight for a while, and I didn't see any side roads ahead, but there had to be. This type of road crisscrossed the Texas countryside, and while it was easy to get lost, it was also easy to get back on track.

I went as fast as I dared, but the pavement was filled with ripples, potholes, and other threats. Mikey sat up.

"What are we doing?" he asked sleepily.

"Running," I said simply just as the SUV reappeared, gaining fast.

We needed to get off this road.

Mikey glanced back, and then opened his phone.

"Half a mile, turn right," he said.

I didn't argue. There was no way I could look at the map and keep us on the road. I had to trust the kid and his instincts.

Harper turned to Mikey. "Do you know where we're going?" she asked.

"Not yet," he said. "Working on it."

Who knew an underage Uber driver might be our salvation?

The right came up quickly at almost a hundred miles an hour, and I braked hard, barely making the turn.

The road was only paved for about fifty yards, and our progress slowed as soon as we hit gravel. We didn't have the tires or the suspension for this. I pushed the little compact car as hard as I could.

But I didn't hold out much hope.

Up ahead, I saw some kind of warehouse-style building, and as it came into view, the road switched back to pavement.

"Mikey, what is that?" I practically yelled.

"Rice and corn farm," he said. "Big one."

A large truck turned out of the driveway leading to the large building, and I swerved around it, turning in.

"I have an idea," I said. "Maybe we can find some help here."

"Help?" Harper asked. "You think some farm workers are going to help us against your sister?"

"Miles," Mikey said. "I think there is something you should…"

But he trailed off as the sign came into view.

Westbrook farms.

My father had a hand in everything.

And we were trapped.

"What are we going to do now?" Harper asked.

"Run," I said.

"Motherfucker!" was her only response.

Harper and Mikey took off at a dead run, and I did my best to follow. I literally hiked up my skirt and ran, finally understanding why women needed to do this. As we reached the building, I yelled, "Harper!"

She stopped and turned, and I caught up with her just inside the doorway. "Give me the drive," I said.

"No," she said. "I have to see this through."

"Let me delay Reanne. Let me take it."

"No. If anyone is delivering this drive to the FBI, it's going to be me."

"Goddamn it, Harper. Why must you be so stubborn?"

Then she grabbed my arm, stood on her tiptoes and kissed me. It took me by surprise, but a second later I was eagerly kissing her back. Our lips pressed together with an urgency I fully understood, and her tongue parted my lips. I sucked in a breath, put my arms around her, and pulled her close to me.

She responded by melting into my arms, and for a moment, the world completely stopped. Then I heard doors slam outside, and I hesitantly pulled away from her.

That second was all she needed. "Good luck, Miles," she said, pulling away revealing my lipstick that was smeared across the side of her face. "When we ditch your sister and finally get out of here, we can continue this conversation."

And she was gone. I waited, feeling ridiculous. She was right, though. If I could delay Reanne and her goons, be a distraction, maybe she and Mikey could make it back to the car and get away. I could join them later once I find them.

But for now, I could be the distraction they needed.

I waited, hearing more noise from outside, and then shouts.

They moved away from me, and I looked across the floor of the warehouse. Crates in huge stacks blocked my view, but I could see the light from outside coming through what appeared to be a large door. We'd entered a side door, and Reanne and her goons entered the main one.

Which meant I was behind them, and they were between me and Harper.

"I see you, Quinn!" I heard Reanne shout. "Get her and that kid, too!"

With that, I broke into a run again, in the direction Harper had gone.

If I couldn't get to her first, maybe I could at least give her and Mikey some help.

I slipped and almost went down, hearing footsteps echoing above. I reached a staircase and rushed up, following the sounds.

I could only hope I wouldn't be too late.

# CHAPTER TWENTY-NINE
## HARPER

I GRABBED MIKEY'S ARM, and we tore through the rows of crates, each one casting eerie shadows in the dim warehouse lighting. My pulse thundered in my ears, drowning out the echo of footsteps that surrounded us. We had to move fast, and my instincts screamed at me to stay low and sharp. This was no time to hesitate.

It was also no time to be thinking of that damn kiss. It was meant to knock Westbrook off guard. Yet here I was, emotionally floored by it.

The irony.

"Keep your head down," I whispered to Mikey, squeezing his arm as we ducked behind a towering stack of boxes. "We're gonna have to get clever if we want to make it out of here."

Mikey nodded, eyes wide but determined. I admired his courage—this was a rough spot, and he was sticking by me without question. As we slid into the shadows, I scanned the rows of crates and boxes, calculating the best way to keep us hidden and cursing the bulky men's clothing I still wore.

Admittedly, it would have been a great disguise if it had even worked for two seconds.

Footsteps pounded down the main aisle, voices getting closer. I peered around the edge of the crate and caught sight of two of Reanne's goons, sweeping their flashlights across the warehouse floor. They hadn't seen us yet, but it wouldn't be long before they found our hiding spot. I took quick inventory of our surroundings, noting a few tools and loose equipment on a nearby shelf. A glimmer of an idea sparked.

"Follow me," I mouthed to Mikey, tugging him along as we crept toward the shelf. I grabbed a length of thick rope and, just a few steps away, found an old fire extinguisher that had definitely seen better days. It didn't smell too great either, so I tried really hard to avoid thinking about where the hell it had been.

I nodded toward an adjacent stack of crates, motioning for Mikey to hide behind it.

The footsteps moved closer, their flashlight beams bouncing off the walls. I took a deep breath, yanked the pin out of the extinguisher, and tossed it under a nearby stack of boxes. The metallic clang was immediately followed by a whoosh of foam and powder that sprayed out in a white, billowing cloud, creating an instant smokescreen. The two goons stumbled into it, coughing and cursing as the fog blinded them.

I moved swiftly, looping the rope around a low-hanging pipe. With a sharp pull, I swung it down, and as one of the goons stepped forward, I yanked it up, tripping him and sending him crashing to the ground. His partner stumbled backward, trying to regain his balance, and I seized the opportunity to dart around them.

Mikey and I sped down another aisle, weaving between the rows as chaos erupted behind us. I heard them shouting, their words muffled by the thick cloud of fire extinguisher powder. I spared a glance over my shoulder and saw one of them rise to his feet, appearing to still be disoriented.

"Harper, this way!" Mikey's voice was barely a whisper, but it cut through my concentration. He pointed to an open corridor of boxes leading toward an emergency exit. I nodded, adrenaline surging as we sprinted toward it.

Just as we reached the halfway point, another figure appeared at the end of the corridor. I skidded to a halt, pulling Mikey back as yet another idiot blocked our path. His sneer was barely visible in the dim light, but the glint of metal in his hand was unmistakable.

"Not so fast," he taunted, lifting a metal pipe as he advanced toward us.

No gun? These guys really were morons.

I quickly scanned the area, my mind racing for a way out. There was a large stack of barrels nearby, and a plan formed. I nudged Mikey, signaling him to stay back, and then I rushed toward the stack of barrels, shoving the top one with all my might and sending it rolling toward the guy's feet.

The barrel crashed into him, throwing him off balance. He stumbled back, his grip on the pipe loosening. I didn't give him a chance to recover. I kicked another barrel, sending it tumbling down the corridor, and it slammed into his shins, knocking him flat onto the concrete floor. He groaned, dropping the pipe as he tried to get up.

"Let's go!" I whispered, grabbing his arm and pulling him past the guy. We slipped through another maze of crates, but my heart sank as I heard more footsteps closing in.

It was only a matter of time before they caught up. We were running out of space to hide. We veered down another row, but this time, the path was a dead end. A solid wall of crates loomed, blocking our escape.

"Damn it," I muttered under my breath, my mind racing for a solution. "Mikey, get down behind those boxes," I said, pushing him toward a small gap between the stacks. "Stay low and keep quiet."

He obeyed without hesitation, his face pale but resolute. I scanned the area, looking for anything that could help us. There was a loose crate leaning against the wall to my left, and I quickly shoved it to the side, creating just enough space for us to squeeze behind it.

The footsteps grew louder, and I pressed myself flat against the wall, holding my breath as more men approached. I saw their shadows stretching across the floor, and my pulse quickened as one of them stepped dangerously close to our hiding spot. I closed my eyes, willing myself to stay still.

But just as I thought we'd escaped detection, a familiar voice echoed through the warehouse, cold and mocking.

"Quinn," Reanne's voice was a venomous whisper, cutting through the silence like a knife. "You didn't think you could hide from me forever, did you?"

My blood ran cold. Reanne was here. I peeked around the crate, catching a glimpse of her silhouette as she prowled through the aisles, her eyes scanning the shadows. Her movements were deliberate, her steps slow and measured. She knew we were close, and she savored the hunt.

I turned to Mikey, my voice barely a whisper. "Stay here, no matter what. Don't make a sound." I handed him the drive and pushed him back.

His eyes widened with fear, but he nodded, pressing himself deeper into the shadows.

I took a deep breath, steeling myself as I stepped out from behind the crate, moving silently along the edge of the wall. If I could create a distraction, maybe Mikey would have a chance to escape. My heart pounded in my chest, but I forced myself to stay calm.

Reanne's voice drifted through the warehouse, mocking and cruel. "You're clever, Harper, I'll give you that. But cleverness only gets you so far. You should have known better than to cross me."

I gritted my teeth, anger bubbling. She had taken so much from me, and she thought she could intimidate me into submission. But I was done running. I was done hiding.

I moved forward, inching closer to her position, when a flash of movement caught my eye. Another guy appeared from the shadows, blocking my path. I ducked behind a stack of crates, but I knew it wouldn't be long before they spotted me.

I scanned the area, searching for anything I could use as a weapon. My hand brushed against a metal rod, and I gripped it tightly, preparing myself for a fight. The thug stepped closer, his eyes narrowing as he scanned the area. I held my breath, waiting for the right moment.

I swung the metal rod, striking him across the back of the head. He stumbled forward, dazed, and I didn't hesitate. I brought the rod down again, knocking him out cold.

But my victory was short-lived. The sound of footsteps echoed through the warehouse, and I turned to see Reanne approaching, her eyes cold and calculating. She held a gun in her hand, the barrel glinting ominously in the dim light.

"Well, well," she sneered, leveling the gun at me. "I have to admit, Harper, you've impressed me. But this little game ends here."

I took a step back, my mind racing as I tried to figure out my next move. But before I could act, Reanne closed the distance between us, her finger hovering over the trigger.

"You thought you could outsmart me? That you could escape?" she taunted, her voice dripping with contempt. "You're nothing, Harper. Just a stubborn little pest that needs to be exterminated."

I clenched my fists, refusing to show fear. "If you think I'm going down without a fight, you don't know me at all."

Reanne's smile was chilling. "Oh, I know you, Harper. I know you better than you know yourself. You've always been predictable. Always so desperate for answers, for the truth. But the truth is, you're just a pawn in a game you can't even begin to understand."

I held her gaze, refusing to back down. "Then enlighten me. Show me just how powerful you really are."

Her eyes narrowed, and I braced myself, knowing that I was out of options. But just as she raised her weapon, a figure appeared behind her, moving silently through the shadows.

Westbrook.

I felt a surge of relief as he approached, his movements calculated and controlled. Reanne hadn't noticed him yet—she was too focused on me, too confident in her victory.

Her finger tightened on the trigger, but before she could pull it, Westbrook lunged forward, grabbing her arm and twisting it behind her back. She let out a furious scream, struggling against his grip, but he held her firm.

"Not today, Reanne," he growled, his voice low and dangerous.

She twisted, and broke free, and she and Westbrook faced off.

Reanne let out a furious snarl, her eyes blazing with hatred. "Let's go, bro. You and me, for all the marbles, just like when we were kids."

He just smiled, and that smile in that moment melted me. "I beat you then. I can do it again now."

Reanne grinned back, setting the gun on a nearby crate. "I've learned a few tricks since then."

They squared off like a pair of boxers or one of those MMA matches, and I held my breath. Mikey came out of his hiding place, and joined me.

Reanne made the first move, and Westbrook retreated.

I held my breath, waiting for him to make his move.

# CHAPTER THIRTY
## MILES

I RETREATED AS REANNE ADVANCED, watching her. She had learned some things since we were kids, with martial arts training and regular workouts. I hadn't been sitting around either, and although I had a bum leg from college ball, I hadn't let it stop me entirely.

As the thought crossed my mind, she darted forward, kicking at my bad knee.

I lifted my foot but her kick still struck my ankle, causing me to stumble. She had some real power there.

As I recovered, I covered my face, and it was a good thing. Two blows struck my forearms, one after the other, promising bruises.

The key lay in my reach. If I could keep her out of my inner circle, she wouldn't be able to hurt me nearly as bad.

I spun and lashed out with a right hand jab, followed by another. That set her back on her heels, at least for the moment. I then pressed forward with a long side kick, causing her to step back again.

She tried to dart inside my reach, and instead of aiming for her head, I delivered a hard and fast rabbit punch to her kidneys. She missed with her defense, and I heard her grunt in response. Instead of dancing away, she spun inside my reach and clocked me on the chin with a hard uppercut.

My jaw snapped shut, nearly biting my tongue, but I tasted blood anyway. I pressed my hand against the top of her head, and shoved her back. She stumbled, and this time I shot my leg out, tripping her and sending her to the ground.

I chased her as if it was a dance. My feet were striking out and missing over and over as she crawled and scampered like a little spider.

She hadn't changed a bit since we were kids, always the slippery one, the only way she ever got the best of me. I tried to stomp on her leg, a sure way to end this fight, but she grabbed my foot and twisted my bad leg. Pain shot from my knee to my groin and I knew something had been pulled or snapped.

I spun on one foot and hopped away. Every time I applied any weight on my left leg it buckled. I held it off the ground, barely letting the toe touch, the only pressure I could stand.

Reanne stood and smiled. "What's the matter, Miles? Something wrong with your leg? If you'd made it to the NFL, we wouldn't even be here, you know that? You'd have gone off to a successful career far away, and the Seagate, and the rest of it, would be mine."

"I never wanted any of this," I said. "But I also didn't want my dad to be a criminal. Or my sister. I just wanted a normal life."

"You could have had it if you'd kept your mouth shut."

As she talked, I tried a little more weight on my left foot, realizing the pain had subsided a bit. Probably a strain or pulled muscle or ligament. Maybe, just maybe…

She darted forward, and I pulled my leg upward with a groan as her sweeping kick went under it. She spun and came again and again.

I avoided her, but just barely. I couldn't keep this up for long, and if she got me on the ground, she had way better grappling skills than I ever had.

Maybe.

Then I had an idea.

"You wanted me to keep my mouth shut," I said as she spun to her feet, but in a crouch, ready to spring. "But I couldn't. Thanks to Harper here, and some others, I saw what was going on. People died for our family's greed, Reanne."

"So?" she chose that moment to spring, and I let myself fall, landing directly on her.

She gasped as the breath escaped from her lungs. She tried to scramble out from under me, but I just let my dead weight rest on whatever part of her body she tried to move. A fist hit me in the eye, but I shrugged it off, using my one good leg to keep up with her as she tried to scramble backward.

She rolled, and pushed, but I kept on, at first trying to trap her, and then just trying to tire her out, which seemed to be working.

"Get her," Harper yelled from the sidelines, and I didn't have the breath to tell her that her cheering really wasn't that helpful at the moment.

Because the effort of tiring Reanne out was working on me as well. My arms could only take so much, and one leg screamed in pain while the other thigh burned with exertion.

Then she was free, and on top of me. Her fists pummeled my body as I hid my face on the dusty concrete floor, my arms over my head to protect it from her blows. I tried to roll over and crawl forward, but she rode me like a bull.

Each of her blows felt a little weaker than the last, but they still hurt, and if she landed one good one in the wrong place…

I dropped my arms, leaving my head exposed for a moment, pressing my palms downward in the push up position. One chance.

I pressed against the ground and got my one leg under me, essentially bucking her off my back. I spun in time to see her foot headed for my face, too late for me to cover.

A second later, she flew across the floor and I turned my head to see who or what my savior was.

Harper Quinn stood there, face red with fury, fists clenched, breathing heavy.

"Sorry, Westbrook," she said, focusing on my sister and not turning her head. "Defeating Reanne is a team sport. Left to yourself, you were losing."

"Quinn," Reanne said, rising to her feet. "It will be my pleasure to destroy that pretty face of yours."

"I'd say the same," Harper said. "But you don't have a pretty face to destroy."

I laughed, and it hurt so bad. I didn't want to tell her how both lame and hilarious her joke was.

And I didn't have time.

Reanne moved, and from my broken perspective on the floor, it looked like a blur. Fists flew, one after the other, followed by kicks and jabs. Somehow, Harper avoided all of them, blocking like a pro.

With all her typical clumsiness, I had a hard time believing she could move so smoothly, but she spun with grace.

One blow landed on her ribs, and I heard her suck in a breath, but other than that the only sound was strikes being blocked and their heavy breathing. Then I heard something in the background, a strange, yet familiar thumping.

Harper advanced. I'd worn Reanne out for her, or so I liked to think, and Harper landed blow after blow. One kick struck Reanne's knee, and she stumbled.

I heard Harper growl. She grabbed Reanne by the shoulders and pushed her back against the crate where my sister had set her pistol.

Harper held Reanne with one arm and punched with the other hand. I saw blood fly from her knuckles as she did.

"This is for Nora!" she said.

"And for Conners!" Another punch

"And Frankie!" Another blow, and I could see she was crying now.

"And Mikey. And me. And all those fucking—" A slap now, and

she switched hands. "People—" followed by another punch. "Whose. Lives. You. Ruined." Each word was punctuated with a blow.

The thumping had gotten louder, but it seemed stationary now, somewhere outside.

One of Reanne's eyes was already swollen shut. The other wasn't far behind, but I didn't think she was conscious anymore anyway.

"Harper!" I said. "Stop!"

She did, her hand held high. Her oversized men's shirt had come unbuttoned at the top, the makeup Luke had used to cover up her feminine features running down her cheeks and over her chin.

Her hair had escaped the hat that was part of her disguise. Tears streamed down her face, blood dripping from her hands down her wrists.

She looked down at Reanne as I heard shouts coming from the open door of the building.

Harper eased her grip on Reanne, letting her slide down the crate to the floor. She stepped back and I went to her, putting my arm around her shoulders. She melted into my padded chest, and ruined my dress with her tears.

It was okay.

I didn't plan to wear it again anyway.

I smiled, kissed the top of her head and held her. I looked over to see Reanne.

One eye was barely open, but she had managed to sit up. In her hand was a pistol, pointed at both Harper and I, amazingly steady.

"You lose, Miles," she said.

I closed my eyes and heard a shot.

Then heard a scream of agony.

I opened my eyes to see Mikey. Reanne's wrist hung, limp and unnatural, and our once Uber driver, now friend, held the gun trained on her.

Harper stopped sobbing for a second and turned around to look.

"Unbelievable," she said in awe.

A second later shouts came from between the crates and dark figures appeared, carrying rifles with flashlights on the end.

For a moment there was some confusion. One of the figures made Mikey drop the gun and cuffed him. The letters FBI were on their backs, and it took me a minute to convince them Mikey was one of the good guys.

Not easy since I was wearing a now bloodstained blue dress.

Fortunately, they cuffed Reanne too, and I figured we could explain her role as well.

Before I could even start, a figure came around the corner.

"Frankie?" Harper said. She moved out of my arms toward the agent, and I missed her touch as soon as she left.

"Quinn," she said. "Looks like you made it."

"I thought you were—"

"I almost was. Mr. Westbrook, I am sorry about Conners. Thanks for your cooperation."

"Thanks," I said. "Nice to see you, alive."

Mikey cleared his throat.

"This is Mikey. He's our—well, he's with us," Harper said. I knew the feeling. I had a little trouble knowing how to describe him as well. Our relationship had become—complicated.

"Nice to see you again, Mikey. How did you hook up with these two?"

Mikey shrugged. "Glad you're not dead," he said.

"Sorry we couldn't get to you in time to save the evidence. We picked up Cameron a little bit ago, but the drive he had on him was nonsense."

"What did you do with him?" I asked.

"We had to let him go," she said.

Mikey pulled the thumb drive from his pocket. "This might help."

"Is that the real thing? Now we just have to figure out the encryption."

"We can help with that, too," Mikey said.

"Um. I'm seriously impressed," Frankie said.

"You should be," Harper interjected. "But how did you know where to find us?"

Then I heard it. The familiar click of heels across the concrete floor. A moment later, Luke appeared.

"Oh, Miles," he said, looking me up and down. "What have you done to that dress? And Harper? My God, what happened girl?"

I stared at him. "How did you—"

Mikey pulled a thin card from his wallet. "I may have programmed the tracker into his phone, thinking we might need some help along the way."

"Thanks, to all of you," I said, pulling one of the crates closer. "But for now, I need to sit down while we talk."

Harper returned and took a seat beside me. She took my hand.

"How about you start at the beginning?" Frankie said, taking a small recorder out of her pocket.

So we took turns telling the story.

"What a mess," she said when we'd filled her in on the larger details. "We'll get your full statements later. Good thing this isn't some kind of fiction story. It would be unreadable."

"You can say that again," Harper said.

"Alright. Let's get you guys checked out at the hospital, and we'll get some other arrests wrapped up once we've had a look at this." She held up the drive.

"Sounds like a plan," I said.

Harper helped me to my feet, and I found myself in her arms, or her in mine. My leg hurt like fire, my arms were lead, and she seemed barely able to hold herself up, so we leaned into each other.

We looked into each others eyes, and I tilted my head down as she tilted hers up. We kissed, gingerly at first, then more intensely. My teeth and lips ached, and I was sure hers did as well, but I didn't want to stop, and her response told me she didn't either. Our bodies meshed for a moment, pressed together as if we, with all our wounds, were one person.

Mikey cleared his throat, and with that we pulled away briefly.

"Harper Quinn," I said quietly. "Will you go out with me?"

"Where?" she said with a lopsided smile.

"I was thinking the hospital for starters. Then we'll see where it goes from there."

"Deal," she said. "But for our second date, I get to wear the dress, okay?"

"Done," I said.

We turned, still relying on each other as we walked outside.

As we emerged from the darkness of the warehouse, the sun struck our faces, causing me to squint.

Harper's hand flew to her temple. "Motherfucker!"

# EPILOGUE
## HARPER

I LEANED AGAINST THE BAR, my fingers playing with the lime wedge in my glass as I glanced around the dimly lit room. To anyone watching, I was just another woman unwinding after a long day. But beneath my loose, casual posture, every nerve was alert, my instincts sharp. My earpiece was barely visible under my hair, and through it, I could hear Frankie, our handler.

"Tell me you've got eyes on our guy," she said.

"Relax, I've got him," I replied smoothly. "The man hasn't budged from his booth. Looks like he's either way too into the game or way too interested in that leggy blonde across the room."

Westbrook let out a small chuckle next to me and took a subtle glance, zeroing in on our target. Thomas Delacorte sat in the corner booth, swirling his whiskey with a look that could've meant anything from irritation to sheer boredom. He was the type who could blend in anywhere, but that night, he was ours.

Frankie's voice buzzed in my ear. She was parked down the street in a surveillance van, coordinating the operation from a safe distance. "Westbrook, Harper—status?"

"We're just waiting for his contact."

"Copy that. Mikey's around the corner if you need an exit

strategy. Remember, we need Delacorte to stay seated until the hand-off."

I heard the low rumble of an engine outside, picturing Mikey's fingers drumming impatiently on the wheel. He had a habit of never sitting still, which drove Westbrook insane. I couldn't help but smile.

"Think he'll ever stop fidgeting?" I whispered, suppressing my grin.

"Only if you let him do a hundred in a fifty-mile-per-hour zone," Westbrook replied, his eyes glinting with amusement as he glanced at me.

The door swung open then, and a man in a black trench coat entered, his eyes scanning the room. He made a beeline for Delacorte's table, not so much as glancing in our direction. Every muscle in my body tensed as I watched him.

"Trench Coat just walked in," Westbrook murmured.

"Frankie, we're about to have a visual on the target's contact," I whispered.

"Copy. Standby."

The man in the trench coat settled into the booth with Delacorte, and the two leaned in close, talking in hushed voices. I resisted the urge to fiddle with the tiny camera hidden in my ring, knowing I'd only get one shot to catch their faces.

"Can we get a visual, Harper?" Frankie's voice broke through.

"Give me a second," I murmured, raising my glass to my lips and subtly angling my hand. The ring caught just enough light to snap the shot. "Got it. Sending it now."

I tapped the button on my bracelet, transmitting the image straight to Frankie's screen.

"Good work," she replied. "Keep your eyes on them. We need to catch the exchange."

Westbrook ordered another drink, leaning over the counter as he kept his gaze trained on the booth. I could feel the tension rolling off him in waves. We'd done this routine a few times already, and I'd learned to read his every move, his every small tell. It was funny—he was the only person I'd ever trusted to have my back, even before I'd admitted it to myself.

The earpiece crackled as Mikey's voice broke in, his tone laced with impatience. "You two better make this quick. My meter's running, and these goons have parked their shiny SUV in my line of sight."

"Foot off the gas, Mikey," Westbrook warned. "Let's avoid the car chase this time."

I barely held back a laugh, exchanging a glance with him. For a brief second, I could see the amusement in his eyes, that same quiet thrill that buzzed through me.

Then Delacorte set a small, nondescript briefcase onto the table, and my heart skipped a beat.

"Now," Westbrook's voice cut through, all business. "That's the signal. When he passes it, I'll intercept. Harper, be ready to run interference."

"Got it," I whispered, my voice steely.

The briefcase slid across the table, and the man in the trench coat took it. Then he stood, glancing around the bar. I felt his gaze settle on us for a split second, his expression tightening.

"Showtime," I murmured, heart thundering as I prepared to intercept him.

Westbrook moved first, heading for the door as casually as if he'd just finished his drink. I took a deep breath and adjusted my position, angling just enough to put myself in the man's path.

As he walked by, I bumped into him, knocking the case out of his grip. He scowled, clearly annoyed as I bent to retrieve it for him.

"Oh! I'm so sorry," I said, smiling sheepishly as I handed it back.

He took the case, muttering something under his breath as his eyes darted past me, no doubt searching for Westbrook. But I held my ground, blocking his line of sight.

That was all the time Westbrook needed.

I saw him make the hand signal toward Frankie's position outside. Westbrook caught my eye and gave me the smallest nod. Message received.

"Move, now," Frankie's voice ordered in my ear, her tone sharp and urgent.

The man turned to leave, but as he reached the door, two agents appeared, blocking his exit. He froze, his gaze darting around, but it was too late. He was cornered.

Frankie entered a few seconds later, her badge glinting under the dim bar lights. "Sir, we'd love for you to join us for a chat."

The man with the briefcase scowled while Delacorte uttered a few expletives from his seat behind us. His scowl deepened as he realized he had no other option.

I let out a breath I hadn't realized I was holding, meeting Westbrook's gaze as relief washed over me. Mikey's voice came through the earpiece, smug and self-satisfied.

"Hope you two haven't forgotten my world-class getaway skills. Vans don't fill themselves."

Frankie chuckled through the line. "You're clear, Mikey. Stand down, everyone. Good work."

As the agents led Delacorte and his accomplice out, Westbrook and I fell into step beside each other, my heart still racing from the thrill of it all. There was something surreal about this new life we'd built, a strange mix of danger and camaraderie that I'd never felt before.

Our fathers and Westbrook's sister Reanne were safely inside Federal prisons, at least for now, probably playing tennis or golf and watching the latest movies on the big screen, but that didn't mean we were safe. Reanne was probably plotting some kind of revenge as soon as they could get enough money to a judge to get their sentences commuted.

We'd joined the FBI in hopes of putting more men like them away and keeping ourselves alive at the same time.

So far, we were pretty damn good at it.

Westbrook nudged me and then leaned in for a soft kiss. I felt breathless as I pulled back, still amazed at the effect he had on me. He grabbed my hand as we stepped outside, the cool night air brushing over us.

"Same time next week?"

I laughed, the tension melting away. "Only if Mikey's buying the first round."

Mikey's indignant voice crackled through our earpieces. "Hey! Nobody said anything about a tab."

But I knew he'd be there, just like always, whether we had another mission or just a round of drinks.

As we walked toward the van, Frankie gave us a nod. The four of us—me, Miles, Mikey, and Frankie made an unlikely team, bound together by circumstance, by purpose, and maybe something even deeper.

Climbing into the van, I couldn't shake the feeling that, for the first time in a long time, we were all exactly where we were supposed to be.

# ABOUT THE AUTHOR

"Making the world a better place by telling stories and helping others share theirs."

Troy Lambert is a freelance writer, author, editor, and publisher who has dreamed of writing books since he was a young boy. He wrote his first book, George and the Giant Castle, when he was six years old. After being told by teachers, counselors, and many people around him that writing was a great hobby but not a great way to make a living, Troy explored other money-making options.

After nearly three decades amassing a collection of name tags, hairnets, and various careers, he finally found the way to fulfill his dream of writing full-time and making a living at it. He currently has written over two dozen books, including ghostwriting projects, and is a freelance writer, content strategist, ghostwriter, publisher, and occasional editor.

Troy lives, works, and plays in Boise, Idaho, with his very talented dog, who is occasionally enlisted to write blog posts and book blurbs. You can learn more about his work at troylambertwrites.com.

facebook.com/authortroy
instagram.com/authortroy
linkedin.com/in/troy-lambert

# ABOUT THE AUTHOR

CJ Rizk is a USA Today bestselling and award-winning author of The Healer and writes under a few different pen names within the romance genre. You can find her sweet romantic comedies of the billionaire variety under the pen name Cynthia Savage, her super steamy scifi romances under the pen name Angelina Avery, and her teen and young adult romantasies under the pen name C. J. Anaya. She holds an AA in Criminal Justice, a BA in Communication, and an MA in Creative Writing/Publishing. When she isn't writing, she's coaching other authors on the book production process and best paths for publishing.

Her personal life can best be described as a mix between the rebooted TV series *One Day at a Time* and *Dog with a Blog*. Her four fabulous children tackle the extraordinary on a daily basis while the family dogs Spike (Pug with an attitude), Lily (Chihuahua mix who couldn't care less), and Grizzy (Pomeranian on crack) continuously remind them that dogs rule and humans drool.

- facebook.com/cjanayaauthor
- instagram.com/authorjourney
- linkedin.com/in/c-j-anaya-author-journey
- tiktok.com/@authorcjanaya

Made in United States
Troutdale, OR
05/09/2025